DANG NEAR DEAD

Also by Nancy G. West

Psychological Suspense

Nine Days to Evil

The Aggie Mundeen Mystery Series

Fit to Be Dead
Dang Near Dead
Smart, But Dead
River City Dead

Aggie Mundeen Lake Mystery

The Plunge
A novella

DANG NEAR DEAD

An Aggie Mundeen Mystery

Nancy G. West

DANG NEAR DEAD
An Aggie Mundeen Mystery

Second Edition 2020

This is a work of fiction. Any references to historical events, real people, or real locales are used fictitiously. Other names, characters, places, and incidents are the product of the author's imagination, and any resemblance to actual events or locales or persons, living or dead, is entirely coincidental.

ISBN-978-1-7341175-5-4

Southwest Publications

Printed in the United States of America

ACKNOWLEDGMENTS

My thanks to these people who graciously contributed to the accuracy of this book.

- San Antonio Police Department Sergeant Devon Lambert who explained death investigations

- Forrest Mims III, for his article in the *San Antonio Express-News* (July 18, 2011) about Texas droughts (www.forrestmims.org)

- Attorneys William Scanlan, Jr. and Daren Digby for information about wills and estates

- Attorney George W. Cowden, III for his knowledge of land ownership and mineral rights in Texas

- Dr. D.P. Lyle, who generously shares his knowledge of forensics with other writers

- Christi Vachon, Bexar County Medical Examiner's Office and Crime Lab

- Pam Scharmen, Bandera, Texas Police Department

- Carey Reed, Bandera Sheriff's Office

- Cindy Martin, Bandera EMS

- Elizabeth Berrien, mystery author and wire expert

- James Kellogg, United States Army, Retired

- Steve Sampson, United States National Guard, retired helicopter pilot

and especially Donald West, who supports my compulsion to write even when it interferes with life, and for taking me to Texarita's Mesquite Grill and Cantina in Bandera before it closed and subsequently burned down.

Any errors that exist in the novel are mine.

I do not, however, accept responsibility for whatever Aggie Mundeen might do.

One

"The trouble with you, Aggie, is you have an aversion to leading a normal life."

Sam Vanderhoven's remark jerked me from my backseat reverie. I'd been contentedly gazing out the windows of his Caprice as it hugged the highway and wound through the gently rising slopes of the Texas Hill Country. Miffed by his remark, I bored eye beams into the back of his head and reminded myself to keep my voice neutral.

"We need a change of scenery... fresh air," I said. "A few days outdoors should do it."

Our friend Meredith Laughlin, sitting in the front seat with Sam, nodded agreement. She'd talked the BVSBar dude ranch into giving us discounts in exchange for writing articles about the place. She probably told the ranch manager I anonymously wrote a column for the San Antonio *Flash-News* and hinted we would collaborate on the articles.

The timing for our getaway was perfect: Meredith and I were out of grad school for summer. She'd been out of college for two years, and I'd been out for fifteen. Hey. Some people are late bloomers. I was finally studying liberal arts instead of business administration and loved being back in school.

From his crabby remark, I figured Sam was still ruminating about the San Antonio health club murder.

Granted, I made his job as SAPD detective slightly more difficult by confronting suspects. When he had to veer from his standard (unimaginative) investigation to try to save my derriere, he developed a dislike for my approach. If we had future occasion to work together, I'd try not to provoke him. He might grow to hate me, and I couldn't stand that.

Meredith and I asked him to join us at the dude ranch near Bandera, Texas, with the stipulation he would come incognito. Nobody at the ranch needed to know he was a San Antonio homicide detective. Having an obvious cop along would cramp our fun. He said it was unusual for police officers to travel incognito, but not unheard of, so he agreed. I anticipated a normal, crime-free holiday.

We climbed steadily on IH 10 northwest going from San Antonio.

Meredith pointed up at the hills. "Look at those trees—hackberries, mesquites, red oaks, live oaks." She'd been researching the area to authenticate her articles. "The Hill Country spans twenty-five counties across an area the size of Virginia. It's filled with lakes and caves and has some of the cleanest air in the country."

When she first mentioned the dude ranch, I'd done my own research. Most articles gave glowing reports of vacationing at the BVSBar, but a couple of articles hinted previous ranch owners died under suspicious circumstances. Maybe it was over-zealous reporting by a neophyte journalist or sour grapes generated by a competing dude ranch.

Meredith pointed. "Those bushy trees are ashe junipers. They thrive in rocky limestone with thin soil and minimal water and actually try to take over the landscape."

Her description reminded me how overwhelmed I'd felt back in Chicago before I moved to Texas: no family, few friends, and smothered with problems—like a defenseless shrub surrounded by ashe junipers.

"Ranchers spend a lot of time trying to eliminate junipers. Texans call the shrub 'mountain cedar' because people get cedar fever from their pollen."

"Nothing like allergies to go along with the heat," Sam grumbled.

He definitely needed time off. This was his first week away from the SAPD since he joined the force—his first vacation since he lost his family in the auto accident three years before. He and his wife Katy had been my best friends back in Chicago. I was "Aunt Aggie" to their daughter, Lee.

Police work kept him busy, and his grief appeared to have eased over time. He probably couldn't imagine lolling around on a vast expanse of land with no investigations to occupy his mind. I hoped our inviting him wasn't a mistake.

Meredith piped up. "Male juniper bushes produce the pollen, Sam, in winter."

I ignored both of them and gazed out the window. Rock cliffs flanked long stretches of highway. Boulders bulged from rising hills. Cenizo, silver-gray bushes with tiny purple flowers, dotted the slopes. From the center of huge yucca plants, cones of white blossoms shot six feet high.

"Thirty million years ago," Meredith said, "an earthquake convulsed this land into hills and valleys." I felt as though we were traveling back in time with hills and boulders blocking us from the civilized world.

"There are a slew of big private ranches around here," she said, "dude ranches like the one we're going to: the Flying L, Rancho Cortez, Mayan, Running-R, Silver Spur, Twin Elm, plus equestrian lodges and hunting camps. Our ranch, the BVSBar, covers eighteen hundred acres."

I couldn't comprehend such space.

We had almost reached Bandera when I read the sign perched on a bluff: "Cowboy Church."

"Bandera says it's the Cowboy Capital of the World," she said. "There's a monument on the courthouse lawn to the world champion cowboys."

We cruised into Bandera and were jarred back into contemporary Texas. We shared Main Street with motorcyclists wearing muscle shirts, jeans and leather. Women riding behind men covered their hair with bandana scarves to protect it from wind and road dirt. Few riders wore helmets.

Midway down the main drag, the Old Texas Square Hotel stretched the length of the block. Texarita's Mesquite Grill and Cantina occupied the center of the building. On Texarita's roof, cowboys sat with their legs crossed and boots hanging over the side. A second look told me the realistic figures were stuffed.

"Perfect," I said, pointing to Texarita's. "Let's eat lunch here."

"The restaurant didn't get great internet reviews," Meredith said.

"This isn't Paris," Sam said. "I'm starved. Let's give it a try."

We parked at the side of the building and strolled into Texarita's front room, a covered patio with a concrete floor and mismatched wood tables. When we sat, a waiter who didn't believe in dental work handed us menus. Sam ordered a twelve-ounce Range Boss Rib Eye. Meredith and I went for Big Bubba Burgers and skipped the forty-ounce Grande Pain Killer frozen margaritas.

On our way to the ladies room, Meredith whispered, "Reviewers wrote service was slow and confused, and the meat was cooked well done, based on some imaginary Texas culinary law."

"Too late now."

"One reviewer said the margaritas tasted like they came from a garden hose."

As we trekked back to the table, a group of bikers walked past and slowed to get a good look at Meredith. They smelled of leather soaked with sweat, tinged with tobacco and peppermint. Sam saw me wrinkle my nose.

"That's Black Jack's Beard Lube," he said, "shaving cream that protects skin from the sun. Some cops use it."

He settled back in his chair. I could sense him relax. After he jailed the health club killer, he had even kissed me.

Those moments were delicious until I considered reality. Sam still grieved for his family. I was skittish about intimacy and burdened with a secret Sam must never learn. Relaxation might smooth our rocky friendship, but we had unresolved issues that could doom a relationship.

When our food arrived, Meredith and I evaluated our hamburgers, took miniscule bites and declared them edible. The meat appeared too old to have beneficial effect. Sam's Range Boss Rib Eye looked like overcooked road kill. He attacked his steak, blissfully unaware.

Meredith looked around. "This motorcycle thing has really taken hold. Some hills around here rise to three thousand feet. The bikers must feel like they're cruising toward heaven."

I felt new enthusiasm for our adventure. I was in good shape from exercising at the San Antonio health club and unexpectedly energized from my Bubba Burger.

"We should walk every morning at the ranch." Exercise was critical to staying young, and I was as old as I planned to get. Almost two-fifths of a century. Gad.

Sam was forty-six. I could deal with an older man, but I knew better than to kid myself. If he learned the truth, he'd shun me like a virus.

I took a deep breath before we climbed into the car. "Unpolluted air. Sunshine. We'll learn to canoe, kayak, ride horses, shoot guns..."

Sam grunted.

"I forgot. You know how to shoot guns."

"Maybe we'll see armadillos, black widow spiders, scorpions, snakes," he said.

"Armadillos are protected by a shell casing of bone over their shoulders and rump," Meredith said. "Flexible bone bands cover their mid-section."

She thrived on precision. After the trauma of losing her husband when he disappeared nine months earlier, she didn't like surprises. When she finally found him, their marriage ended. Except for her compulsion to be precise, I thought she was recovering.

Sam was thinking about armadillos.

"There've been times I sure could've used that body armor. Texas has a variety of snakes, right?"

Was he determined to make us anxious?

"Yes, but only two species are venomous," she said. "Coral snakes and pit vipers like rattlesnakes, copperheads and cottonmouths. The red-yellow-black on coral snakes looks similar to colors on harmless snakes. What you watch for is red touching yellow."

I didn't plan to get close enough to a snake to watch for anything. My enthusiasm dimmed.

Meredith spread out a map and pointed ahead. "About two miles beyond that hill, we should be at the ranch." She checked her watch. "We should arrive at 1:45 p.m., in plenty of time to get settled before evening activities."

She navigated life via research, planning and timing. At only twenty-four, she had developed amazing organizational tendencies. After she lost her husband, an event she couldn't control, she apparently became determined to program her environment to make that awful tragedy her only lifetime slip-up.

Still, she's the sister I'd like to have, even if she is fifteen years younger than I am, smart, blond and beautiful.

I suppose I'm smart enough. In looks, I'm slightly above average. Slip-ups in my life are common and continuous.

"I've made enough notes about the terrain," she said. "I'm ready to see the ranch."

We topped the hill and saw the entrance gate, bracketed on both sides by an eight-strand wire fence. A four-by-eight-foot wood plank sign hung between wide gateposts. BVSBar Ranch was scorched into the wood. When our front wheels bumped over the first iron pipe of the cattle guard, the gate swung open. A winding ranch road curved ahead. Sun sparkling on limestone crushed into dirt beckoned us toward whatever lurked around the next bend. Even Meredith was too captivated to worry.

"Wow," she said. "Perfect."

"Must be the Western White House," Sam said. We drove on a road barely wider than our car. Live oaks, mesquite and black brush flanked our vehicle, hiding wildlife I knew must be there.

A cow lounging in the road ahead swiveled a sullen face toward us, her loose jaw chewing her cud. As we rolled closer, she lumbered to stand, focused on us with disgust and took a firm stance in front of our vehicle.

"She's chewing curly mesquite," Meredith said. I thought she was mostly slobbering.

Having apparently concluded that we'd fatally interrupted her reverie, the cow swiveled around, flipped her tail at us and waddled into the brush.

Meredith giggled. "I hope the people are happier to see us."

We rounded a bend and saw ranch headquarters. The lodge made of Hill Country limestone with a steep metal roof stretched wide across a clearing. The wood-plank porch, bordered with a stripped cedar handrail, wrapped around the building.

Sam eased his four-year-old navy blue Chevrolet, a 1993 Caprice he bought from SAPD, up to the porch rail. The vehicle looked so much like a cop car, he might as well put a sign on it. Maybe Bandera County residents wouldn't notice. Sam parked next to a yellow Jeep CJ that looked like it had bumped over a lot of rocks.

He got out, hitched up his pants and slapped the Caprice's hood. "Wonder if I oughta tie this here doggie up for the night?"

Meredith and I smirked. As we climbed onto the porch, I spotted Sam's new Roper boots. He must not be totally opposed to country life. I missed a step, bumped into a cedar post and scratched my arm.

"Ouch."

"Are you okay, Aggie?" Sam always appeared amused by my tendency to crash into inanimate objects. I ignored him and reached for the lodge door.

Angry voices coming from inside the building froze my hand on the knob.

Two

"Whadya mean you went horseback ridin'? You're assistant manager, for chrissake." I gathered the woman with the husky voice was the manager.

"Have you inspected the cabins for guests comin' in? Did you stop by the waterfront and shootin' range to see if the wranglers are ready? Did you check the stables or just nab your horse and take off? You're s'posed to be helpin' me." She sounded as though she didn't need much help.

I heard a softer, less strident female voice. "Those women in cabin six are too busy twittering over cowboy sightings to want anything else. There's no way I can clean in there anyway. Their clothes are strewn all over. If I go anywhere near cabin four, Selma Tensel lectures me about conservation like she discovered it. George Tensel, the old coot, ogles me when I leave."

"What about the corrals?"

"Ranger Travis doesn't need any help. He's got Monty to do his scut work. Besides, I don't like milling around among loose horses inside a corral. It's dangerous. And I don't like the way Ranger leers at me."

The manager's voice rose. "Then stay away from Ranger. Get those empty cabins ready. We got people comin' in."

I knocked twice and opened the door. When I peered in, the older woman's face was flushed.

Both she and the younger woman pasted on smiles. "Bertha Sampson," said the first woman. She emerged from behind the check-in desk and stuck out a rough-skinned hand for us to shake. "Manager of the BVSBar Ranch. Welcome to God's country."

Bertha could have been in her early forties. Meatiness distorted harmonious features that I thought had once graced a thinner face. Her eyes might look huge if not sunk in puffiness as they were now. She wore a loose western shirt hanging over baggy jeans and well worn, flat-heel boots. Her hair looked as if it received the same lack of care as her clothes.

I silently pledged to keep exercising, avoid salt, and wear flattering attire.

"This here's Vicki Landsdale, my assistant." Vicki, who looked about twenty, had pale blue eyes and a rosebud mouth. Her fair skin and strawberry-blond hair made her appear way too delicate to exist on the rocky terrain we just navigated. We shook hands all around like settlers reunited after surviving a journey through the badlands.

Meredith signed the ranch guest book, paid for our rooms and smiled at the women as though they were old friends. "This lodge is lovely. How old is it?"

"It was built in 1865. The thick walls keep us from needing much air conditioning," Bertha said proudly. "Beams and porch rails are made from stripped cedar trees right off this ranch."

From what I'd overheard Vicki say, conservationist Selma Tensel, in cabin four with husband George, would have preferred they left the cedar trees in the ground.

"Rock paths and steps are all made of Hill Country limestone," Bertha said. As she described the ranch, her face softened. "Vicki, honey, show these lovely folks the way to their cabins." Bertha nodded to us. "She'll get you whatever you need."

Vicki led us down the steps and gave Sam driving directions to our cabin.

Meredith hopped into his car. I told Vicki I'd walk with her and follow them. I like getting to know people and trying to determine what makes them the way they are. Sometimes I get so curious, my feet itch.

We started down the trail. The two o'clock sun beat down on us as we shuffled along the limestone and dirt road. The temperature felt like it was above ninety, but the air was dry and the sky clear.

I filled my lungs.

Whitebrush alongside the road blocked our view into the thicket. I thought I heard small animals skitter away. There were no guest cabins anywhere. No other people. I needed to talk.

"Have you been assistant manager here long?"

"Sometimes it seems like forever," Vicki said. "I wasn't doing very well in college in Wisconsin. I started dating this guy...a hippy-type sociology major/artist with long hair." She shrugged. "Big deal. My parents pegged him for a loser and wanted to get me away from him. Since I like horses, they thought a summer working at a Texas dude ranch would make me appreciate what I had back at school. So they got me this job, shipped me down here and hoped I'd be ready to return to college in the fall."

Most contemporary parents gave up worrying about their kids' college friends. Either Vicki's parents were old-fashioned, or her family was exceptionally close. I found their concern refreshing, not having had a real family myself. Anyway, it sounded to me like the girl could use a friend. Long walks make people open up. I still couldn't see any cabins and was beginning to sweat.

"He was a nice guy," she said. "Had a lot of empathy for people."

I sensed Vicki had the same trait.

"His sociology class used to visit war veterans at the Milwaukee VA hospital. He took me with him a few times." She stopped, looked at the sky, took a deep breath and visibly settled down. "It's so peaceful here."

Peaceful but hot. I heard another critter scurry through the brush.

"Probably a mouse," she said. "We don't see very many. Snakes or hawks generally take care of them." My skin prickled.

"You're sure it was a mouse?"

"A larger animal like an Angora goat or white-tail deer would have made more noise. Deer hide in the brush all over the ranch. We have to confine Angoras to fenced areas on the northwest side of the property; otherwise, they eat all the vegetation. We have javelinas, but they forage at night. They look like pigs and travel in bunches. You usually smell them before you see them. They have a musk gland near their tails that smells awful."

"And you like it here?"

"It's not so bad. I love being outdoors, and I've found a great horse to ride."

Our feet made a scratchy sound on the path. Sometimes I'd see the hint of a building, but when the trail turned, it would disappear. I felt as if we were alone in the universe.

"It's good to get out from under my parents' thumb," she said. "They're good people, but they can be overbearing. They thought I'd hate this place. Actually, I like being on my own. Some of the guys here are jackasses, but most of them are nice." When she blushed, I wondered which nice wrangler she had in mind.

"I miss having somebody I can talk to," she said. "I hope you don't mind."

"Of course not. I love meeting new people."

"I've never been anywhere but Wisconsin. At nineteen, it's time I looked around. If I just didn't have to deal with Trey..." She looked out at brush as dense as her thoughts must be. I waited for her to elaborate. Trey, whoever he was, apparently wasn't going to be a topic for discussion.

"Is your work hard?"

"Not really. When we have a full complement of guests and some of them are demanding, we get pretty busy. Most of the time, I get to enjoy watching people have fun. Bertha's loud, bossy, and short on social graces, but she's a good manager. I've learned a lot from her."

"She seems to love this ranch."

"She managed guest services for her aunt and uncle for years. She knows every inch of these eighteen hundred acres."

We were isolated in the middle of a big chunk of land. I had researched the layout of the ranch. Except for roads leading to the main lodge, cabins, or areas used for activities, this whole eighteen-hundred acres was rough, rocky country covered with thickets of mesquite, whitebrush and cedar where deer and other hardy creatures could roam, hide and proliferate. The soil couldn't sustain farming or grazing; it could only support sheep and goats. As Vicki said, the manager had fenced off an area where her Angora herd could eat everything from wildflowers to weeds without stripping the brush white-tail deer needed for cover. I found Bertha Sampson listed among Angora goat breeders. She apparently exploited every conceivable route to make her acreage profitable.

Vicki was talking. "Bertha's the one who found them...her Uncle Max and Billy Sue Vernon."

I stopped. "Found them? What do you mean? What happened?"

"She found their bodies in a remote area of the ranch five years ago, dead from heat stroke and dehydration. Their Jeep was nearby, out of gas. It's the yellow one Bertha parks near the lodge."

The articles I read held some truth. "Surely they took water."

"They knew to take water. They grew up in the Hill Country and appreciated the power of the Texas sun. Bertha said the sheriff found their empty thermoses. Max collapsed near the car. Billy Sue apparently tried to walk back to the lodge but didn't make it. They were in their late fifties. The last time Bertha saw them, she said they were giggling like kids and said they were going on a treasure hunt. She had no idea what they meant."

"Do you know?"

"I've never heard any talk about treasure."

"Were they in good health?"

"Bertha told me they exercised regularly. Billy Sue was determined to stay young and was always going to some diet meeting. Max was careful about what he ate, but I heard he took pills for something."

My empathy mushroomed. In spite of all they did to take care of themselves, the Vernons died way too young.

"Bertha must have been devastated, finding them like that. Did they have children?"

"They had a son, Herb, who never cared one whit about the ranch. He's married now, but they rarely come around. Bertha was like the Vernons' daughter. They left the ranch to her. Their will said she shouldn't sell it to a developer, but she wouldn't do that anyway. Her soul is here. She wants everybody to care about this place like she does."

"The medical examiner must have done autopsies?"

"I guess so. Bertha doesn't talk about it. She still drives their Jeep, though."

"The one parked in front of the lodge?"

"Yes. She tells everybody it's her personal vehicle, off limits. But she leaves the keys in it. I think it's her way to remember them."

Just beneath my sympathy for the Vernons and for Bertha, my curiosity bubbled. Unexplained deaths would undoubtedly pique Sam's interest, even deaths that occurred five years earlier. It appeared the reporter who wrote about the Vernons wasn't overzealous. Maybe he hoped to prompt an investigation of their demise.

Our vacation might not be peaceful after all.

Three

While I debated when to tell Sam and Meredith about the former ranch owners' deaths, we arrived at cabins five and six, which were enclosed side-by-side within a single elongated building.

"You and Ms. Laughlin have cabin five," Vicki said. "There's a breezeway running behind both cabins' sleeping areas and a community bathroom behind that. The three girls have the cabin on the right, cabin six."

"Girls?"

"We call them that. They're actually three women who've never been in the country before."

Her description sounded like Meredith and me. I was clueless about outdoor living except for my brief childhood time at Uncle Fred and Aunt Novena's farm outside Chicago after Mom and Dad died. Meredith, a native Texan, was a city girl, but she did have experience riding horses with English saddles.

Sam had mentioned traveling to Wisconsin to hunt and fish when he lived in Chicago. After earning English and law degrees, he joined the FBI. Shortly after he and Katy married, he left the FBI to become a homicide detective for Chicago PD. He said he preferred local law enforcement.

Since moving to Texas, he hadn't had time for outdoor recreation.

He pulled the Caprice up to where the road stopped a hundred feet in front of our cabin. Between the cabin and Sam's parking spot, a huge live oak tree with a ten-foot diameter canopied over a picnic table. At the edge of the canopy, paths snaking right and left wound around to cabins barely visible in the distance. Ranch buildings were apparently widely spaced. Secluded. Meredith's and my cabin must be pretty far from Sam's.

She and I grabbed light suitcases from the trunk and plodded toward cabin five with Sam toting our heavy bags. Vicki held the door open while we stepped inside to peruse our accommodations.

Our habitat looked to be about fifteen by eighteen feet with two stacked wood bunk beds angled together at each corner. Filling the wood bed frames were thin yellowing mattresses, a far cry from the pristine white bedding we were used to. Meredith frowned. At the right end of the room, a wood table and four chairs filled the center space between corner bunks.

"I can use that table for my laptop." I'd learned the ranch had recently gotten dial-up internet service. For readers who wrote Dear Aggie seeking advice on staying young, I researched techniques and products that promised perpetual youth. I continued writing the column anonymously when I moved to Texas, but I wanted to get in the best possible condition before revealing my identity. Nobody wanted a slightly overweight, out-of-shape slob pontificating about how to stay young.

We asked Sam to heave our suitcases onto chairs and eyeballed bunk beds in the left corner.

"Two bottom bunks?" I said.

"With double sheets on the mattresses." Meredith turned to Vicki. "Could you get us a couple more sheets and four pillow covers?"

"Sure."

Lower walls around the cabin were made of cedar planks turned rough side out. They'd never been sanded or varnished. If we brushed against them, we'd get splinters. Above a waist-high rail, unpainted wood ran up to the low ceiling. There was a window at each end of the elongated cabin. The floor was stained concrete. A few braided rugs might have softened the effect. The open doorframe at the rear of the cabin apparently led into the breezeway and, beyond that, the community bathroom. The entire structure seemed designed to make occupants long to be outside.

"We'll tour the ranch later and enjoy dinner and music on the patio." Vicki handed us maps of the ranch showing locations of the lodge, cabins for guests and staff, the Medina River where we'd swim, corrals, and the shooting range. The brochure had looked like a pleasant summer camp for grown-ups. Now I realized we were actually going to engage in physical challenges.

Vicki pointed to a spot on the map. "If you walk back toward the lodge, you'll see an arrow sign on a tree directing you left toward the river. I'll meet you at the waterfront at three-thirty."

She turned to Sam. "While they settle in, I'll show you your cabin, Mr. Vanderhoven. You're in cabin four, next to Selma and George Tensel."

"The conservationist? That might be interesting." I smiled innocently. I was still irritated by his remark about my aversion to normalcy.

He swung around and tramped toward the car to get his suitcase, looking grumpy. I usually ignored his irascible moments, but I was worried. He could easily descend from grouchiness into depression. Meredith sensed my unease.

"He'll be all right. As soon as he gets used to the environment and slower pace, he'll begin to enjoy himself."

When Sam's precious daughter, Lee, died with Katy in that terrible auto accident, a chunk of my heart died, too. Sam grew so depressed that six months after they died, he escaped to Texas.

Months later, when a huge banking conglomerate bought the small bank where I worked, and my bank stock shot sky high, I had options. The aunt and uncle who reared me had passed on, so I had no ties to Chicago. Texas sunshine might be what I needed. I moved to San Antonio and enrolled in graduate school to study everything I missed the whole time I was submerged in banking and business courses. That's where I met Meredith.

When Meredith's husband disappeared and her life was threatened, she called SAPD, met Sam, and the three of us were thrown together. Before that, I hadn't seen Sam for over two years.

I prayed this vacation would lift his spirits. His hike to cabin three hauling luggage was not apt to be pleasant, stuffed as he was with Range Boss Rib Eye. I hoped Meredith was right. Once Sam settled in, he'd relax.

Meredith and I evaluated our abode.

"Pretty primitive." I poked at a mattress. "Squishy."

She pointed at shaky wooden nightstands at the foot of each bunk. "Those might be big enough for a paperback, book light and Kleenex. We can stack shoes on the bottom shelf." She looked around for closets. "Where are we supposed to put our clothes?"

"Must be in the bathroom."

She followed me through the doorframe into the breezeway that ran across the building. Beyond the breezeway was the community bathroom. Inside, long counters running down the left wall held four wash basins with spigots. I hoped they produced hot water.

On the far wall of the bathroom, two shower stalls flanked two toilet cubicles. I whooshed open a white rubber shower curtain. A plastic showerhead loomed high over a drain in the concrete floor. A shelf on the shower wall held a bar of lye soap. A cheap plastic chair rested against the shower wall.

"Plush."

I peeked behind the rubber curtain of a toilet cubicle. It had its own floor drain and prison-quality toilet paper. Forget privacy. Noise would carry across the concrete like shots over water... another reason to appreciate the outdoors.

"I bet this hut's creepy at night," she said.

"Uh-huh. And if we leave the light on in the bathroom, we'll never sleep."

She pointed at two metal hanging racks on rollers standing in the breezeway. "I found the closets." The racks looked like thrift-store contraptions. Our suitemates had already hung clothes on them. One batch consisted of gauzy flowing garments in neon colors. A second clump of clothes included jeans and T-shirts. The third bunch of garments was composed of western garb, complete with silver buckles and turquoise necklaces. "The 'girls,'" I said.

At the end of the breezeway, wooden boxes jutting from side walls formed square cubicles with plywood bottoms. Our suitemates had stuffed several squares with toiletries and left some empty cubicles for us.

"Our chests of drawers?" I said.

"Right."

We heard a raucous laugh, a shrill giggle, and metal jingling from the direction of cabin six.

"Time to introduce ourselves?" I said.

Four

Meredith shrugged, but I knew she was as curious as I was about whoever went with the clothes.

Chubby arms jingling with charm bracelets protruding from a floating tent of gauzy iridescent orange swept into the breezeway. The Camping Angel? Bleached hair tied high in a pom-pom bounced above crinkly, kohl-rimmed eyes and fire engine red lips.

“Well, hellooo,” the apparition said. “We thought our suitemates would never come. I'm Jan Meisner, ‘Jangles’ for short.” She fluttered her hands, tinkling enough gold to set off metal detectors across the county. She slid over, graceful on espadrilles, her huge bosom bouncing under flimsy fabric, and grabbed our hands. “Isn't this just the most beautiful place? Ever since I sold my Ft. Worth beauty shop, I've wanted to come to the Hill Country.”

The country might not be ready for Jangles, but her enthusiasm was contagious. We barely had time to introduce ourselves before a glow of southwestern turquoise flashed into the bathroom hanging on one of Jangles' roommates.

This woman gleamed like a drugstore cowboy. Her ranch-style shirt had pearlized buttons down the front and on pockets and cuffs. She had managed to stuff herself into new jeans. A tooled leather belt with a shiny turquoise and coral buckle cut her ensemble in the middle.

“I told Jangles not to wear those floatin' hostess pajamas,” she barked. “This is a ranch. If she gets near brush, she'll get snagged and leave half herself in the bushes. I'm Rhonda Stone. They call me Stoney. If we're going to fit in at this ranch, we need to dress like it. We don't want these ranchers to think we're dudes."

Stoney shook our hands like she was pumping a well. Meredith smiled, her mouth slightly open. For once, I was speechless.

"Stoney was one of my customers at the shop," Jangles said, as if that explained everything. "She likes to dress for the occasion. She's determined to get this cowgirl thing right. I just like to be myself." Jangles giggled, flouncing her top and tinkling her trinkets.

We heard a shriek from their cabin and rushed in to find their third roommate cringing on top of the wood table, clasping her knees. "There are bugs on my mattress! I looked on the back side and there they were. I'm sure they bite. How can I possibly sleep on that foul pallet?"

"Get over it, Mildred," Stoney said. "We'll knock 'em off your bed." Stoney turned to us and spiked her thumb toward the agitated woman. "This is Millie Dietert. She's never been outside Dallas."

"With good reason," Millie whined. "No wonder rural Texans are strange. They bed down with creatures."

"Millie came to my beauty shop, too," Jangles said.

Meredith told them our names and approached Millie's mattress.

She studied the surface and gingerly turned the mattress over. "No black widows or brown recluses. Just a few Scorpion remnants. Dead. A cockroach wing or two. Few doodle bugs. You're good."

Millie paled.

"When they air out the cabins," Meredith explained, "a few bugs probably get in and try to hide under mattresses. But they die from the heat. Vicki missed a few when she cleaned everything. Nothing there's going to hurt you. Your friends can help you air out the mattress. Vicki's bringing extra sheets. I'll give you one of mine."

Meredith could deal with bugs. She had studied them. It was the unknown that scared her.

Millie sighed. She helped Stoney and Jangles haul her mattress though their front door, whereupon Stoney delighted in flipping off critter remnants. Jangles and Stoney hoisted the mattress back to Millie's bunk while Millie swallowed a Valium and watched.

Meredith assured Millie it was safe to sleep on her mattress.

I said I needed to check my email before we toured the ranch.

"Be sure and wear ranch clothes," Stoney called. "We're going to the waterfront, the firing range and the stables."

My baggy jeans, blue denim blouse and tennis shoes would have to do. Gad. We were actually going to swim in a river, ride cow ponies and shoot guns. Was it too late to back out?

I tried not to dwell on what lay ahead. I turned on my laptop and waited for buzzing phone clicks to connect with the internet. A Texas dude ranch in June seemed the perfect place from which to advise readers how to stay fresh, beautiful, and young in summer while frolicking outdoors in a hot, hostile environment with Texas wranglers and unknown critters. A challenge. Since I'd slid pretty far past thirty, staying young topped my personal list. Helping readers avoid the ravages of age reduced my deep-seated fear of crashing into middle-aged decrepitude.

The *Flash-News* would forward me letters addressed to Dear Aggie, and I'd email answers back to the paper for readers with critical problems. The newspaper would save less urgent questions and answers to print in my weekly column.

I waited for the search engine to find the *Flash-News* site, hoping I wasn't making final contact with the civilized world. Clicking on "Stay Young with Aggie," I entered my password and found a letter addressed to Dear Aggie. The letter didn't appear to be an emergency. This reader had a few days to plan:

Dear Aggie,

My new husband wants me to go camping with him in a state park. In a tent. As a child, I camped in the back yard until a bird pooped on me, and I ran inside. Now that I'm mature (not old), I don't think I'm cut out for outdoor life. What should I watch out for?

Fearful in Ft. Worth

Dear Fearful,

Hopefully, you selected a husband who will sleep in a tent only on top of an inflated mattress. After he struggles to set up the tent and creates a frenzy inflating your rubbery bed, you'll both be ready for a slug of wine. You'll probably watch the sunset. Until he wants to try out the mattress. Here's where you have to take a stand. In your absence, critters might have tested your comfy abode. Insist that Hubby lift the mattress, shake it and turn it over. While he does that, ogle the inside corners of the tent. Sleeping in the midst of unknown creatures causes premature wrinkles, aging, and stress-induced hardening of the arteries. If you see a black spider with a red spot on its abdomen (black widow) or a brown spider with a darker brown mark that looks like a violin (brown recluse), urge Sweetheart to call the nearest motel. If you see only crickets and doodle bugs, ask Hubby to throw them outside, put sheets on the disgustingly primitive pallet and attempt to sleep. Forget romance. Sweetheart may not understand your reluctance, but if you're lucky, he'll never ask you to sleep in another tent.

Always Alert,
Aggie

Having helped my first reader navigate the challenges of summer and pleased that I'd helped her avoid an age-inducing camping fiasco, I shoved toiletries into a bathroom cubicle and bath linens into another pigeonhole. When I washed my face, a fine layer of dust transferred to the washrag. It hadn't rained in Texas for a long, long time.

I freshened up, listening to Millie berate her roommates. "I can't believe I let you two talk me into coming to this wilderness." Hopefully, our experience at the ranch would prove better than Millie expected.

Brushing my hair, I fluffed it with my hands and looked forward to introducing the girls to Sam. Before dabbing on makeup, I put on sunscreen, determined not to let the Texas sun age me. I applied lipstick, wondering how Sam had fared with his suitemates. Even though he implied I was abnormal simply because he didn't understand my sleuthing methods, thought he knew everything and was grumpy, I found it hard to stay mad at him.

When Meredith was ready to go, we crammed empty suitcases under our bunks, walked outside to sit at the picnic table and waited for Sam to walk with us to the waterfront. Our suitemates trudged out of the cabin and joined us.

Stoney jerked her chin toward Jangles. "We made her take off those espadrilles."

Jangles held her foot up. She wore flip-flops with a V adjacent to her red-painted big toe. Over the V lay The State of Texas, outlined in rhinestones. She tittered. "Aren't these perfect?"

"River Rat will love 'em," Stoney said.

At the mention of River Rat, the women perked up. Squealing and jingling, they headed for the river.

Sam trudged from the direction of his cabin toward Meredith and me, shuffling once-shiny boots though the dust. Selma and George Tensel, Sam's suitemates, walked several yards behind him, conversing loudly.

When he reached us, Sam flipped his thumb in their direction and muttered under his breath, "Those people jabber all the time. It's like living next to chimp chatter at the zoo. Selma nags George to immerse himself in activities while George complains about the ranch. He says it's too damned hot in Texas in June to frolic outdoors."

George had a point.

Sam heaved a sigh. "It's going to be a long vacation."

My mouth turned up at the thought of Sam's suffering through his suitemates' chatter. I'd wait a while before telling him and Meredith about the dead ranch owners. I'd never admit it to Sam, but with unexplained deaths lurking in the ranch's past, I was glad he came. If problems arose, I didn't think our suitemates would be much help.

I turned a bright smile on him. "Let's go to the river. Water is always calming."

Five

We checked the map Vicki gave us and pinpointed the walking trail that went from our cabin to the lodge. Heading toward the lodge, we saw a wooden arrow nailed to an oak tree with "Swimming Hole" burned into it. We turned left and merged on to a dirt trail covered with horseshoe tracks, probably a trail-ride route. Rocks bordered both sides. The horse trail extended east and west in both directions. A line of mesquites interspersed with oaks on the far side of the trail indicated we must be near the Medina River.

We crossed the trail, stepped over the rock border, walked toward the waterfront and discovered an oasis. Bald cypress trees flanked the Medina River, their limbs overhanging the banks. Pecan trees towered near the edge. Oaks stood farther back, as if standing watch. Soft grasses, poking around outcroppings of limestone, swayed toward the water.

"The short grasses are grama and buffalo. The tall grass is bluestem," Meredith said reverently.

A tall, tanned male stood at the end of a dock that extended out into the water with his back to the river. His black eyes matched long jet-black hair tied at the end with a piece of rope. His mane shone like it was perpetually wet. His bronzed chest rippled with muscles. Lycra swim trunks hugged him two inches below his navel to his knees.

Our suitemates had arrived. They sat a few feet in front of him on the dock, staring up at water god as if mesmerized in worship. Jangles' gauzy fabric flounced around her on the dock like a parachute.

Stoney sat to one side, dangling a bootless foot defiantly in the water. She looked as if the water god didn't hurry and make his speech, she would jump into the river. Millie sat as far back from the river as she could, sneaking glances at the green water as though it concealed the murky depths of hell.

Water god smiled at each woman in turn, his black eyes penetrating each one's gaze like missiles hitting their mark. When we approached, he cut black-bead eyes to us and checked us out: Sam, the Tensels and me. Then his eyes rested on Meredith.

Sam stepped around fabric and appendages, extended his hand to water god and introduced us.

Water god smiled. "Trey Harding," he said. "Around here they call me River Rat."

When Vicki sauntered up behind us, River Rat gave her a perfunctory nod.

Rat bared perfect teeth. "Welcome to the BVSBar Ranch. In this beautiful Medina River, you'll paddle through sun-twinkled water and secluded shady groves. You'll swim like minnows." I hadn't expected River Rat to be a poet. Vicki didn't seem impressed.

Millie looked terrified. "Are there big fish in there?"

River Rat ignored her. "Tomorrow morning, come in swimsuits." He beamed at Meredith, probably imagining her in a string bikini. "You'll get in, a few at a time, with everybody wearing lifejackets. I'll divide you into groups: tadpoles, frogs, and fish."

"If we need life jackets," Stoney said. "I was a lifeguard."

Rat didn't respond. "Tadpoles will get used to the water in shallow areas," he said. "You'll slip in, jackets on, and swim to various points. I'll swim with you." He smiled.

I hoped he had a life jacket big enough for Jangles. Maybe her boobs would float.

"Frogs swim with and without jackets. Fish try out the canoes and kayaks." He pointed to boats lying on the grass by the river.

Meredith, Sam and I were good swimmers, so we "fish" would probably learn to steer watercraft. I had swum with Sam and his wife Katy at the exercise club in Chicago. Meredith and I had used the health club pool in San Antonio, but swimming in a river would be different.

Sam whispered, "I'm glad I can swim. He probably saves only women."

Eyeing the grin on water god's face, I decided that steering a canoe would definitely be preferable to frolicking in the water with River Rat.

Selma Tensel piped up, "Are there any endangered species in there, like the Texas salamander?"

"What's a salamander?" Millie squeaked. "Is it big?"

"For Pete's sake, Selma," George muttered to his wife. He turned to Millie. "It's a brown thing five inches long that lives in caves and eats whatever flows in because it's blind." Selma glared at him.

"Those little guys prefer the pools in the San Marcos River," Rat said. "We have ordinary critters here."

Millie paled. "What kinds of critters?"

"Nothing to hurt you, Sweetheart," said River Rat. Millie appeared too panicked to appreciate his attempt to flirt.

Sam leaned toward me and whispered, "Good thing he didn't mention water snakes, western cottonmouths, rose-bellied lizards..."

"Shush, Sam. She'll hear you." With all the noise and splashing we'd make, I didn't think a snake or lizard would get anywhere near this crowd.

Jangles flashed a Cheshire Cat smile at River Rat. "We'll be just fine with you helping us and all, won't we, Sweetie?"

He grinned. "Sure thing. Any more questions? No? Then I'll see y'all in the morning."

While Jangles heaved herself and her parachute up from the dock, Stoney dried her foot and stuffed it back into her boot. Vicki pointed the way to the stables.

"Walk to the right," she said, "behind the lodge. You'll see glimpses of the firing range in the distance on your left and the corrals straight ahead." She looked irritated but was apparently trying to hide it.

I let everybody walk on ahead and waited for her. "River Rat sure knows how to charm the ladies."

"Yeah." Vicki lowered her voice. "I can't believe the women in cabin six go nuts over him. They can hardly wait to get him in the water. 'River Rat' fits him, the big creep. His last name isn't Harding. He's my sorry brother, Trey Landsdale," she whispered. "Nobody here knows that, so don't say anything."

With Trey's dark skin and hair, and Vicki's fair skin and strawberry-blond hair, nobody would guess they were siblings.

"My parents stashed him here to spy on me," Vicki said. "What a joke. They don't realize what a screw-up he is. He's the one who needs to get his life straight. When I caught him forging a check on my account, I told him there'd be no more smoking weed and drinking on my dime. I wonder what he does with guests in that river. Maybe he shares his booze and marijuana."

"Good grief. Won't Bertha find out?"

"Eventually. He's pretty smooth, but one of these days, he'll make a guest mad. I'd like to be around when Bertha finds out about his doping and drinking. When our parents shipped him here, he figured he had them fooled, and he could mooch off me easier. He has his own trust fund, what's left of it. I couldn't believe they sent the creep to watch me! That was the last straw. How was I supposed to trust him or my parents?"

She glanced ahead to make sure her charges were still walking toward the stable. Their footprints obliterated horseshoe tracks on the trail.

Vicki moved over to whisper in my ear. "I told Trey I might take a hike and disappear. I liked it here until he showed up. As far as I'm concerned, he can wallow here forever. If I leave, my trust fund goes with me." She looked back to make sure Trey wasn't around. "When I told him that, he got so mad I thought he was going to capsize one of his stupid canoes and hold me under it. He's always had a temper."

This girl definitely needed someone to confide in. "Do you really plan to disappear?" I knew what it was like to be without anybody to rely on. The uncle and aunt who raised me in Chicago died soon after I turned eighteen. That's when I got my job at the bank. It wasn't good to be alone. Maybe that's why I was so eager to latch on to Lester, the first and only boyfriend I ever had. I was so eager to change everything. Eager to escape. Eager to permanently belong to somebody. Eager to seal a relationship with sex.

It took me a while to figure out that sometimes it's better to be alone.

"Disappearing would be cool," she said, "like in a witness-protection program. Trey threatened to tell Mom and Dad I want to leave the ranch. If he does, they'll probably show up and insist I come home." She lowered her voice so I could barely hear. "I've already transferred some funds. I'll need untraceable money to support my untraceable self."

"You sound serious. What about Bertha and your horse and the people you like?" There was apparently one wrangler she would miss.

"I will miss them." She looked sad but resolute. "But it's time for me to be free."

Why did I sense that, despite her urge to be liberated and her secretive plans, she'd never really be free? She reminded me of myself at her age. Desperate to fly, but clueless about which way to go. She seemed to trust me. Maybe I could help. Somehow.

"We're almost to the stables," she said. "I need to walk on ahead. You won't repeat any of this?"

"Of course not. Let me know if I can do anything." She needed a mother figure to talk to. Even though I was obviously much too young to be her mother.

Six

We approached the corrals. A skinny cowboy perched on the top fence rail with his legs bowed around a post. His Stetson dwarfed his head.

"Welcome, folks. I'm Monty Malone. I worked rodeos afore Ranger Travis said I oughta work here." He pointed to the lanky, big-shouldered cowboy inside the corral whose hat didn't quite shade his chiseled face. When the rugged cowboy tipped his hat above his six-foot-four frame, the girls murmured. His half-shy grin and thick lashes stirred even my stomach. Ranger Travis might be the cowboy Vicki hated to leave.

When Ranger looked at Vicki, his grin widened. She stared pointedly at the horses. Monty watched their exchange with a satisfied expression before he shimmied down from the fence. I sidled his way in case he made any interesting observations.

Ranger started his spiel about the horses. About that time, Bertha sauntered up. As she watched Ranger, her face softened and her eyes grew round.

"We have thirty-five horses in this corral," Ranger said. "You can ride most of them, but we keep a few back for ranch hands. We'll match you with the best horse for you. They're all gentle, but some of 'em have quirks. Some don't like halters, like Scooter over there."

He gestured to a dapple-gray mare with a black pigmented circle around one eye. The sun probably reflected differently off that circle from the way it bounced off gray skin around the mare's other eye. Scooter probably saw things differently from each eye: with a halter coming toward her, she might perceive a misshapen foreign object that looked monstrous.

"Some of these horses," Ranger continued, "will take off if you dismount and let the reins drag the ground. You can wrap the end of the reins around the saddle horn or, better still, hand them to a wrangler. Another thing, when you're trying to get on a horse, make sure you mount from the correct side."

Ranger should have specified which side of the horse he meant. Millie's eyes were like saucers.

"Sassy over there"—Monty pointed at a short, stocky mare with a stiff mane flopping around flinty eyes—"she blows up like a balloon when she's cinched."

"Then what happens?" Millie asked.

"You get on and start goin' good," Monty said. "Then Sassy farts the air out. All of a sudden, the saddle's not cinched tight enough to stay on her. You slip off sideways with the saddle." He slapped his knee and guffawed.

Millie turned pale.

A big-boned black horse ambled toward the fence where she stood outside the corral.

"Don't feed that one," Monty said. "He bites." Millie jumped back two feet. Sam chuckled.

"Yeah," Monty added, "and don't ever rein Dime too hard or he'll pitch you in the dirt."

"Which one is Dime?" Millie squeaked.

"That paint horse over there." He pointed to a horse that looked like somebody had doused him with cans of brown and white paint.

Ranger shot Monty a stern look. "Don't mind him. He gets a kick out of hasslin' new riders."

Monty pouted.

"We'll catch your horses for you," Ranger said. "It's not a good idea to walk in here among 'em. If they're not sure what's coming up behind 'em, they might spook."

"Spook," Millie said. "You mean snort and look wild, like they do now?"

Monty gestured toward a tall horse and muttered to Millie under his breath, "You come up behind Marbach—that brown gelding over there that's sixteen hands high—he'll kick the crap outta ya."

Millie's hands started shaking. Horses plodded aimlessly inside the corral.

"They're just milling around," Ranger said. "They sense you're new people and think they're going to be ridden."

The women cringed outside the fence. Sam winked at Meredith.

"We'll start slow," Ranger said, "until we're all real comfortable. For riders who learn to ride good enough to go on the trail ride"—he eyed each woman, including me—"I'll make something special for you. A souvenir of the ranch." He lifted a multi-strand ring of wire. At first, I thought it was barbed wire, but it was thin and without barbs.

"Since we use a lot of wire on this ranch, I decided to make things with it. I can't sing country western, so I do this." Ranger moseyed over to a cardboard box, swaggering like Clint Eastwood. He hummed Brooks and Dunn's "A Man This Lonely" while he pulled wire sculptures attached to wooden bases out of the box. I recognized one creature as an armadillo. The other sculpture was a bald eagle landing. Ranger's wire creations were amazingly lifelike.

The women tittered, except for Vicki. A cowboy built like a fullback who had an artistic side had probably appeared in most of their dreams.

"Ain't he great?" whispered Monty, keeping his voice low. George Tensel gave Monty a look of appraisal.

"I usually like horses better'n people," Monty said, "'cept fer Ranger. When I worked that rodeo circuit, I was sleepin' in one stall and shovelin' out the rest when Ranger come along." Monty peered at me from under his hat. "I hope you don't mind my talkin'," he said. "We ain't had many guests for a while."

"I understand. I enjoy listening."

Ranger passed his sculptures around for everyone to admire.

"This job is better than the rodeo circuit?" I asked Monty.

"Best job I ever had. When Ranger said he needed a wrangler at this here ranch, I jumped at the chance. I've done ever' thing from dodging snakes to shoveling shit. This job is easy: no traveling...steady work...having one boss—well, two, countin' Bertha Sampson. It beats having ever' cowboy and rancher in a hunnert miles telling you what to do."

He lowered his voice. "I'm not countin' Bertha's assistant as my boss. Vicki's nothin' but a citified twit. Beats me why Ranger cain't see it. Ever time Ranger eyeballs Vicki, ole Bertha expands like a blowfish. It's obvious the old bag has the hots for Ranger. If Ranger don't quit chasin' after Vicki, he's liable to lose his job and mine along with it. That snippy girl needs to get lost."

I didn't think Vicki was one bit interested in Ranger. She was probably contemplating her best time to escape.

Sam and Meredith, bored with Ranger and his sculptures, strolled over toward Monty and me. I told Monty how much Sam loved horses and dude ranches so Monty would keep talking.

"When Ranger offered me this job, I told him right off about getting drunk and hurtin' that twerp," Monty said.

My ears perked up. Sam moved closer.

"They said I hurt the guy pretty bad, but I don't remember nuthin'," Monty said. "Ranger said everybody makes mistakes. He gave me this here job in spite of everthing."

Sam narrowed his eyes. "You recently hurt somebody in a fight?"

"Aw, no. It was a long time ago. Probly ten years. That feller's bound to be healed up by now."

Sam studied Monty and didn't reply. I glanced up in time to see Ranger smile seductively at Vicki. Bertha frowned.

"Come on, everybody. Time to go to the firing range," Vicki said. "Thank the wranglers." She started the group clapping, let them pass by her and pointed them toward the next stop.

Monty caught up to George Tensel and started chattering. I guess Monty figured he'd worn the rest of us out. George was probably ready to listen to anybody who didn't talk about conservation or nag him to exercise.

"You go on ahead," I told Meredith and Sam. I was convinced Vicki needed someone to talk to. My feet had started itching ferociously. I wanted to know what Vicki thought about Ranger Travis. I caught up to her and walked alongside. "That wrangler's really handsome," I said. "Talented, too."

She shrugged. "Ranger's good looking, but he's all show. Bertha makes a fool of herself drooling over him in his skin-tight jeans. If he flirts with me, she always seems to notice. Monty doesn't like Ranger paying attention to me either. He's not about to let anybody get near his meal ticket. I finally had to tell Ranger to buzz off. He looked mad enough to charge me with his horse. Monty needs to quit worrying about my latching onto Ranger Travis. I want somebody with brains."

Vicki didn't seem to be interested in anybody at the ranch. She and brother Trey were at odds. She didn't like Ranger, and Monty didn't like her. Bertha was usually mad at her. There must be somebody she cared about, somebody she hated to leave. I just hadn't met him yet.

"Who's in charge of the firing range?"

"Wayne Rickoff," she said. "He's a Vietnam vet who spent time in a Wisconsin VA hospital. Once, before shotgun class started, I caught him aiming at one of the horses, then at Ranger. When he saw me looking at him, he whirled and put me in his gun sight. He lowered the gun right away, but he had a wild look in his eyes. He gives me the creeps. What did I ever do to him?"

"When your boyfriend took you to the rodeos in Wisconsin, did you see a lot of angry vets?"

"Not too many. Some of the older vets, maybe in their forties, seemed especially angry. I was told they served in Vietnam."

Since when was forty old? Vicki was too young to remember, so I told her what it was like for soldiers in Vietnam. "When they came back from combat, many soldiers felt the war provided no resolution of conflict for anyone. Regardless of how they responded, the outcome seemed to be an endless stream of casualties with no results. And people booed the returning soldiers."

"Wow. No wonder they were angry."

"Yes. Regardless of how hard they worked, sweated, bled, or how many friends they saw die, the outcome was the same. Our GIs were constantly rocketed or mortared, but felt they gained no ground. When they returned to the US, they tried to put together some positive reasons for that time in their lives. But they found very little support from friends and neighbors at home."

"I know that feeling," she said.

"I'd see Vietnam veterans at the bank where I worked in Chicago," I said. "They looked depressed, hopeless, angry. Some were irritable and easily startled. They'd have sudden outbursts of anger. The war affected many that way, either from what they'd seen or personally experienced. I read about post-traumatic stress disorder so I'd know how to relate to them."

"When Rickoff pointed his gun at me," she said, "he looked like he was ready to attack."

"He might have hallucinated that you and Ranger were enemies, Viet Cong. That's a symptom of PTSD: trauma from the war come back, triggered by some unforeseeable event or person, and they're ready to fight again."

"What awful symptoms to live with," she said. "I hope that's not what Wayne Rickoff is going through."

Vicki definitely had a kind heart. But she didn't seem to have a single reason to stay at this ranch. With all the animosity floating around, I wondered if we should leave. Two unexplained deaths had occurred here, Vicki's doping brother was trying to steal from her, and she was desperate to escape. Monty had hurt somebody during a drunken brawl. Wayne Rickoff was an unpredictable war veteran who might suffer from PTSD and randomly pointed his gun at people. If I told Sam about

Rickoff's gun incident, he would have Meredith and me packed up and back on the highway in thirty minutes.

I had counted on this vacation. Sam needed more time to heal. We needed time together without a crime to solve and a slew of cops and suspects around. We needed just enough time together. Not too much time. After my ghastly experience with Lester, I had mixed feelings about everything, including sex. Being loved (or so I thought) and left by Lester had affected so many people: me, Sam, his wife Katy, the child.

If I could help Vicki, maybe she wouldn't flee. I knew from experience, after Lester took off, that merely running away wouldn't help. Instead, I worked my way up to bank vice-president and earned a business degree at night. But I grew desperate to leave my boring job and Chicago's lousy winters.

When I moved to San Antonio, I was financially secure for the first time. Free to live anywhere. And young enough to start over. When San Antonio's *Flash-News* said they'd run "Stay Young with Aggie," that cinched it.

I thought, when we are all together in Chicago, that I was falling in love with Sam. Single and thirty-nine, it was time for me to go to Texas and find out.

On vacation, we had the chance to become reacquainted. Despite conflicts at the ranch, I decided to wait awhile before telling Sam everything I knew.

Seven

Vicki turned our group around and led us back past the stables. We walked so far, we couldn't even hear the horses. I guessed the shooting range had to be a good distance from the ranch's populated areas in case somebody fired in the wrong direction.

My watch showed it was approaching five o'clock. Scorching sun seared the back of my neck. My dry mouth told me the temperature must be mid-ninety.

George and Selma Tensel padded behind Vicki. Selma periodically pointed out cenizo, black brush or a red yucca plant.

"Who cares about plants?" George said. "I need air conditioning, a cold shower and a beer."

Our suitemates walked behind Selma and George. Jangles waddled and puffed with sweat dripping down the back of her neck. The Texas rhinestones covering her toes were dirt brown. Stoney strode with by-god determination, whacking mosquitoes. Nobody remembered to bring bug spray.

Millie looked despondent. I heard her talking to herself. "I haven't seen one activity that looks safe."

Sam, Meredith, and I walked far enough behind everybody to avoid their dust. Sam craned his neck around Meredith to peer at me. He raised an eyebrow: "Are we having fun yet?"

I wrinkled my nose at him and kept walking. I cajoled him into coming to the ranch by hinting that, although a dude ranch didn't appear to be dangerous, two unarmed women traveling alone might need protection in the middle of eighteen hundred remote acres. He couldn't resist my logic. I hoped my lame excuse didn't prove true.

When the firing range came into view, Vicki turned around and walked backward, gesturing behind her. "This is where we learn to trap shoot. We fire shotguns at moving clay targets as though we're firing at game birds. Our instructor, Wayne Rickoff, is a Vietnam veteran and crack shot who wins skeet shooting competitions."

Vicki obviously couldn't reveal more about Rickoff, or her charges would scatter like mice. I didn't know his entire history, yet I couldn't help but feel apprehensive.

We moved toward an area ringed with benches in a half circle. Off in the distance, waist-high tripods placed thirty feet apart held round four-foot-diameter targets. Rickoff stood with one foot on a bench, a shotgun resting across his thigh, and stared glumly at our dusty herd of approaching novices.

"This is Captain Wayne Rickoff," Vicki announced. He nodded. No change of expression. "Monty's setting up the trap machine," Rickoff said. "I'll show you how to hit those bulls-eyes out there.

"Cover your ears."

He took his stance, aiming at the round, padded targets. They were painted with concentric rings in different colors with red bulls-eyes in the center. Rickoff fired shots at each target and moved to the next. When he was through, each bulls-eye had fresh holes torn through its center.

Sam muttered under his breath. "Damn."

"Can you do that?" I asked.

"Not that well. Not without practice."

Goosebumps raced across the back of my neck. If Sam grew worried, I'd freak out.

Rickoff continued shooting. We saw Monty way off in the distance to the right.

A new man sauntered up to our group. He wore earphones under his cowboy hat and had his face painted like a clown. Ranch guests turned to look at him. When the barrage finally stopped,

Vicki introduced him. "This is Sunny Barlow, camp cook and singer." Her delivery was more animated than usual. Barlow smiled and welcomed everyone to the ranch.

"Sometimes I clown at rodeos," he said, "and occasionally, I clown for kids. Hope you don't mind my wearing clown makeup here at the ranch." We all shook our heads. He exuded charm.

"It takes a while to put the face paint on," he said. "Sometimes I get last-minute calls. This way I'm ready to go."

We nodded. When Sunny Barlow smiled, you couldn't help but smile back. I squelched the urge to go over and hug him.

"I like to watch Rickoff shoot," Sunny said. He nodded to Vicki, stuck his hands in his pockets and turned to watch the show.

When Jangles maneuvered closer to him, he lifted one earbud. "You're going to cook dinner?" she asked. "Tonight? On a campfire?"

"That's right. It'll be cooling down soon. Sunset should be beautiful."

"You're the one who sings, too?" Millie inched toward Sunny in her first spontaneous move since she leaped onto the cabin table.

"That's me." His clown smile grew wider. He had the kindest eyes. I wondered if Vicki knew if there was some other reason he wore a disguise.

Rickoff stood with his gun shouldered. "Y'all want to see this trap shooting or not?" he barked. In the distance, Monty worked his way into position, ready to start the trap machine.

Rickoff turned toward him.

"Pull," he yelled. Monty yanked a lever. A clay target shot high in the sky and arced to the left. Rickoff blasted it to smithereens. He shouted again, "Pull!"

The bombardment continued for five or six volleys until Rickoff yelled "Pull," and nothing happened.

"Dang thing's broken again," Monty yelled. Rickoff cursed.

"I brought some minis just in case," Monty shouted. "I'll throw 'em up fer ya."

At Rickoff's command, Monty threw up three smaller clay targets in succession. Rickoff pulverized them.

I heard Jangles whisper to Stoney, "I've got to go to the bathroom. It's too far to walk back to the cabin."

"Go out there in the bushes," Stoney murmured, "way back behind us. Get far enough away so you can't see us."

"I couldn't possibly..."

"Nobody can hear a thing. Give me those bracelets. I'll watch where you walk and mark your direction."

Jangles slipped off her trinkets, handed them to Stoney and headed for the brush. The women instinctively closed rank with our backs to her so the men wouldn't see her leave.

"Pull!" Rickoff shouted. Monty threw up a clay target, and Rickoff blasted it. They repeated the stunt for a good ten minutes. My ears rang. I was amazed at Monty's ability to toss clay disks in the right place, time after time, and in Rickoff's ability to annihilate them.

A cool breeze blew through our ranks. Sam sidled close. "It's great sharing my vacation with a crazed sharpshooter." He winked at me. At least his sense of humor had returned. If he knew the veteran's whole story, he wouldn't be joking.

Rickoff turned to reload. He was apparently going to impress us with another feat.

Monty came loping up. "I'm out of minis. I'll get more in town later." Rickoff looked disgusted. He probably could've shot all day.

Somebody screamed.

Rickoff and Monty leaped backward. "A snake!" someone screeched.

Monty zoomed to the nearest fence and sprang to the top in one jump.

Rickoff fired his gun over our heads.

Jangles crashed out of the bushes and came stumbling toward us, pulling up orange gauze bottoms.

"Somebody's shooting at me," she shrieked. The flimsy fabric on her flailing arms snagged every bush she passed.

Sunny Barlow stood closest to Rickoff. Millie, intrigued by Sunny, had managed to inch up beside him. A red, yellow and black snake slithered two feet in front of them.

Rickoff aimed at the reptile. He looked like he was about to pull the trigger when Millie whimpered, fainted, and fell on top of the snake. Its head poked out from under Millie's rib cage. We froze, terrified it would bite her. It wriggled out from underneath her and slithered toward the brush.

"Let's get her up," Sam said. He and Sunny pried Millie's limp form off the dirt and hoisted her to her feet. Supporting her dead weight between them, they maneuvered her back toward the road, trying not to wake her up until they could distance her from where she collapsed on the crawler.

Jangles struggled to pull up her gauzy pants. She stared at the spot where the snake was last seen and started to hyperventilate. Stoney ripped shredded fabric from Jangles' mangled sleeves and fanned her with it.

"It's going to be okay," Stoney said. "Take a real deep breath. That's it. Let it out slow."

"Dang it all," said Rickoff, "I hate coral snakes." He scratched his head and squinted. "Coulda been a scarlet king."

Everybody whirled and started walking at a good clip toward the lodge.

Curse words spewed from the men. Thoroughly shaken, Meredith and I tried to catch up.

Sam and Sunny were still holding up Millie. She was regaining consciousness when Jangles and Stoney overtook them.

"Thank you, guys," Jangles said, red-faced, with shredded clothes and blackened feet. "We'll take care of her." She and Stoney got on either side of Millie. "She'll be all right, won't you, Mill?" Jangles said.

"Just an accident," Stoney said. Millie nodded, her jaw slack.

"This is outrageous," Selma said.

Stony and Jangles talked into Millie's ears so she couldn't hear the others discuss what had happened.

"They should capture these snakes and put them in a zoo where they belong," Selma huffed. "They're not supposed to be out here scaring people to death."

"They live here, Selma. It's their habitat," George blared.

"Shut up, George." Selma stomped ahead. "If you'd been as close as I was to that slimy creature, you'd have died of a heart attack."

"I can't believe this happened," Vicki said. "I haven't seen a snake the whole time I've been here." Jangles and Stoney kept talking to Millie while we trudged through the heat. Sunny starting singing Reba McIntire's "How Was I to Know?" By the time he finished the song, everybody had grown quiet except Vicki.

"I'm in charge of you guys," she said. "I'm supposed to make sure we're always standing in a cleared area. We were in a cleared area. I don't know why the stupid snake was even there. Bertha's liable to fire me on the spot."

I insisted what happened wasn't her fault, but she peeled off on a side path with her head hanging. "I'd better go to the lodge to make sure everything's ready for tonight's barbecue."

Sunny Barlow watched her go. He'd already removed his ear protectors. He took off his hat and ran his fingers through black curly hair. "Let's not mention what just happened to Bertha...okay, everybody? We might get Vicki fired," he said. "Nobody wants that."

We might not have heeded his plea, except for his winsome smile. Who can resist a clown? Several people mumbled, but I thought they'd keep quiet about the incident, at least for a while. The heat and snake had sapped the fight out of them.

Vicki was succeeding at the ranch, despite having made enemies, but her luck couldn't get much worse. Her lousy brother saw her as a meal ticket. He apparently wanted to demean her to their parents and steal her trust fund.

Bertha fussed at her, and Ranger Travis and George Tensel leered at her. Sunny Barlow seemed to be the only person at the ranch who gave a flip about the girl.

Vicki was trying to find herself, like me at her age. I believed Lester and I truly loved each other. Until he took off. When Aunt Novena and Uncle Charlie died, I was eighteen with no place to go. Sam and Katy Vanderhoven were wonderful, but they didn't know what happened with Lester. I'd been deserted. Katy was the only one who knew about the baby. When I told her, all our lives changed.

I understood why Vicki felt the need to disappear. And now this snake incident. In the pit of my stomach, sadness and unease welled up for Vicki Landsdale.

Our prospects for a peaceful vacation did not look promising.

Eight

We approached our cabin. After I watched the girls go inside, I signaled to Sam and Meredith we needed to talk. I wanted to update them in case something really bad happened. After Selma and George passed us and were beyond earshot, I spoke in a whisper. "This place may be more than we bargained for."

I told them Trey was Vicki's brother with a fondness for drugs, alcohol and her money, and that Vicki felt the need to disappear to get away from him.

"She also said Bertha's aunt and uncle, the Vernons, died five years ago in a remote corner of the ranch from heat stroke and dehydration. They left Bertha the ranch, which didn't sit well with the Vernon's son, Herb, even though he never liked living here. Vicki also said Bertha and Monty resent it when Ranger Travis flirts with her."

"Looks like there's more sneaking around here than snakes," Sam said. "There might be more to Monty's story about attacking that guy. Then there's Wayne Rickoff."

I relayed Vicki's account of Rickoff's pointing a gun at a horse, then at her. "Vicki said he spent time at a VA hospital."

"He seems so angry," Meredith said. "I think he's scary. Maybe we should leave this place. I wish I already had enough material for my articles."

Sam's brow furrowed. "Looks like Rickoff wouldn't mind lining up guests for target practice. It's unusual for a skilled shooter to fire off a gun in the middle of a crowd to scare a snake."

"Vietnam must have made him jumpy," I said. I didn't mention Rickoff might suffer from PTSD since I didn't know for sure. Now that Sam and Meredith knew about Rickoff's actions, I thought I should try to find out more about the veteran before labeling him. "Did you bring your gun?" I asked Sam.

"Yep. Baby Glock's in my pocket. I carry it when I know there's going to be firearms around. A .27 is easy to conceal."

"Did you consider shooting the snake?" Meredith asked.

"I didn't want to advertise I was armed. Besides, people worry me more than snakes. I think we should cut this vacation short."

"Some of these people might need help," I said. "Don't you think we should stay a while longer?"

He frowned and looked off into the brush.

"Poor Millie," Meredith said. "Thank goodness that snake didn't bite her."

"Maybe it was stunned. Did you see its shiny mouth?" I said.

"Probably the sun reflecting off white scales," Sam said. "Okay. I'll keep my eye on Rickoff and River Rat. Right now I'm going to clean up." He tromped toward his cabin.

It appeared we weren't leaving the ranch. At least not yet. Having told them everything I knew, I felt safer. Sam was armed and would watch the men. The other wranglers seemed more intriguing than dangerous.

I was learning to enjoy being in the great outdoors and looked forward to watching sunsets with Sam. And I was determined to find a way to help Vicki so she didn't feel compelled to leave.

Meredith and I noted Jangles' blackened rhinestone flip-flops on their front porch and traipsed through our cabin and the breezeway to check on the girls. Stoney was patting Jangles' scratches with a square gauze soaked with rubbing alcohol.

"Whooeee, that stings."

Jangles had showered off sweat-streaked make-up and powdered her cheeks, which were still beet red from her sprint through the bushes. She'd captured her clean hair with a rubber band and poofed it into a beehive. Her soft flared jeans and flat-heeled boots looked serviceable. She wore a blouse with long sleeves she could roll down to cover her scratches.

Stoney's teased and sprayed hair reminded me of a prickly pear bush. Her earrings, necklace, and belt shone with enough coral and turquoise to impress Mayan royalty. I hoped she didn't have to run anywhere. The weight of her jewels would slow her to a crawl.

"Where's Millie?" I asked.

Stoney pointed up toward the corner. Millie lay prone on her top bunk with her arms and legs flopped over the sides. "Says she needs to rest," she whispered. "We didn't tell her when she fainted, she fell on a snake. We suggested she shower and put on jeans and a wrinkle-free shirt before she crawled up there. We'll wake her up in time to primp for the barbecue."

Meredith and I left our suitemates and returned to our cabin. I told Meredith that while she showered, I needed to check my email for letters to Dear Aggie.

Before I went to work on my column, I wanted to research Trey Landsdale. It occurred to me that if Vicki's brother abused drugs, he might have a criminal record.

My WebCrawler search indicated he had none. His clean record made it more reasonable their parents would send him to watch over Vicki. If they believed he had only minor problems, they might think giving him some responsibility would straighten him out. Maybe they realized Vicki was the stronger of the two children.

Yet, I still had misgivings about River Rat, Trey Landsdale. Since he'd grown up in Wisconsin, I looked up the state's marijuana laws: possession of marijuana was punishable by six months in jail and/or a fine of $1,000 for the first offense. Conditional discharge was available for first offenders. Subsequent offenses incurred three-and-a-half years in jail and a fine of $10,000.

Suppose authorities had previously caught Trey with marijuana. The Landsdales might have paid the $1,000 fine and had him conditionally discharged.

At that point, they might have suggested he adopt a different name and get a job in Texas at the dude ranch where Vicki worked.

He could keep an eye on his sister and keep himself out of jail.

In Texas, possessing marijuana incurred 180 days jail time and a $2,000 fine. Two to four ounces drew a year in jail and a $4,000 fine.

Possession or sale of stronger drugs carried greater penalties in both states. Trey Landsdale must have known that if he went to Texas, he'd have to be very careful. If he got caught using illegal substances, his parents might balk at paying the price of keeping him out of jail.

On the other hand, the Landsdales might prefer having Trey jailed in Texas. They'd have a better chance of keeping his misdeeds out of the Wisconsin papers.

I still had time to check my email before dinner. Sure enough, somebody had written to Dear Aggie.

The paper would have to email her my answer. This reader needed advice fast.

Dear Aggie,

Our friends have a ranch. They insisted we visit them. Dinner and camaraderie were great, but tomorrow we're going on a three-hour hike. I'd just as soon jump off a cliff, but I can't get out of it. Any suggestions?

Creeped-out in the country.

Dear Creeped,

First, wear cool, comfortable clothing with a sweater and COMFORTABLE walking shoes. No boots you haven't broken in. Don't even consider flip-flops or espadrilles. High-topped tennis shoes are good. If you wear regular tennis shoes, stuff your jeans into tube socks. Wear sunscreen and a hat. You don't want to survive outdoor life only to look like a hag. Use bug repellant. Mosquitoes either love you or hate you. Why chance it?

I know you're thinking about snakes. Most are not poisonous and avoid people. If that doesn't make you feel better, wear gloves and sprinkle granular Snake-Be-Gone around you as you walk. Or sprinkle it on your shoes.

Better still, walk in the open. If your host starts to walk though brush, walk directly behind him.
Remember: heat, Deet, and feet.

Aggie

I was glad we weren't taking any prolonged, age inducing hikes. I could hardly wait to get the dirt off, even in a primitive shower using lye soap. Fortunately, I discovered I'd packed a bar of Ivory.

Meredith and I were in our underwear, mid-way through blow-drying our hair when the power went out in the building. Cabin electricity apparently couldn't support two hair dryers. We groped around in semi-darkness, trying to find clothes that matched.

Millie's voice carried through the breezeway. "Is it almost morning? I had a terrible dream about a snake." In loud voices, as though they had to shout to be heard over the darkness, the other two girls explained the electrical malfunction to Millie, reoriented her to pre-dinner time and didn't mention the snake.

When Sam banged on the front door, the lights came on. "Are you ready to go eat?"

"Y'all go on," Jangles called. "We'll get Millie ready and be there in a minute."

Meredith opened the door. "We had to dress without lights," she told Sam.

"I spent the last hour listening to George and Selma Tensel argue," he said. "George hates everything about this place. They don't serve liquor, so he had to drive to Bandera for booze. He hates having to walk everywhere. Selma harped he needs more exercise but pointed out he has no trouble chasing young girls like Vicki."

"Ouch."

Poor Vicki. This was one more conflict she didn't need.

"George thinks it's stupid to see grown women panting over a bunch of tight-butt, small-brained cowboys," Sam added.

Meredith grinned at me. There are some things only women appreciate.

"George also despises the indignity of having to heave himself onto a horse," Sam said.

"Did Selma say that's another reason he should exercise?" I asked.

"Right. He also hates stripping to a swimsuit to dunk himself in a river. Selma reminded him he used to say he loved the Texas Hill Country. She grew euphoric talking about its natural beauty. When she started pontificating about conservation, I had to get out of there."

Sam wore a long-tailed shirt hanging out over his jeans. He must be hiding the Glock.

We strolled toward the main lodge, listening to blessed silence. I saw two small buildings secluded in the brush off to our left. From having studied the ranch map, I thought the first cabin, closest to ours, must be Vicki's. Through the window, I saw a blouse draped on a chair.

Farther down the road, I concluded the building closest to the lodge must be Sunny Barlow's cabin; it had the initials "S. B." on the door.

As dusk crept around us, the cicadas tuned up. "What are those? Locusts?" Sam said.

"Texans call them cicadas," Meredith said. "They invade in June and stay all summer. Males make those sounds by vibrating the membranes on their abdomens."

"Maybe George Tensel will take that up instead of snoring. He snores so loud, he rattles the pipes in the bathroom."

Cicadas surrounded us from trees everywhere, chirping a rhythmical strain as if they were celebrating the day and preparing the countryside for nightfall.

"Do cicadas have any natural enemies?" he asked Meredith.

"They lay hundreds of eggs in scratched-out areas of tree bark. When their offspring, called nymphs, fall to the ground, they frequently land near cicada-killer wasps."

We seemed to have landed in the middle of vast acreage that concealed mysterious deaths, conflicts between people, siblings with issues, a man hiding behind a happy face, a veteran who probably suffered from PTSD, and snakes.

Yet the sky shone with more blue, pink, and orange streaks than I'd seen in any other sky. The air smelled purer than I'd imagined air could smell. The tone of humming cicadas enveloped us in a blanket of sound lulling us into security. How could anything go seriously wrong in such a place?

Nine

To the right of the lodge, a large concrete patio was set back alongside the building. A breeze rustled red and white checkered tablecloths covering cypress picnic tables spaced across the concrete floor. Cicadas sang hymns to the streaked sky. I inhaled the fresh air.

Sunny stood on the patio beside the outdoor fireplace, stirring coals. “Come on in. While we wait for the coals to heat up, I’ll sing.” He sauntered to the nearest table, heaved a foot on the bench seat, laid the guitar across his thigh and began to croon “Country Roads.” Even the cicadas grew quiet. Sunny smiled at our suitemates when they walked in, and they rushed to the table nearest him.

Sam had captured the table to Sunny’s right and spread himself out on the bench seat so Meredith and I could sit opposite him. Since the ranch wasn’t full, there were tables left over. Sunny wore subdued clown makeup and no hat. We had a good profile view of his strong, regular features. Why would he want to hide them?

Bertha came out of the lodge carrying a tray of steaks. Vicki followed, struggling with a platter of baked potatoes and a mammoth salad bowl. About that time, Ranger Travis swaggered in wearing chaps, as if he’d spent the day riding a cutting horse through the brush.

Sunny grinned and broke into “Momma, Don’t let your Babies Grow Up to Be Cowboys.”

"You got that right," Bertha said, winking at Ranger.

Ranger tipped his hat to each woman. We all checked him out as he strolled around and spoke to everybody. He slid onto the bench at a center table.

When Sunny stopped singing to put steaks on the grill, Ranger requested "When Will I Be Loved?" Sunny started the song, and Ranger was ready. He cocked his head back like a howling coyote and sang loud, harmonizing with Sunny: "I've been cheated...been mistreated. When will I be loved? I've been put down; I've been pushed 'round. When will I be loved? When I find a new girl that I want for mine she always breaks my heart in two. It happens every time... I've been made blue, I've been lied to. When will I be loved?"

By the time they got to the last line, every woman in the place looked ready to volunteer to help one or both men feel loved.

Vicki's brother slipped in and slouched at a table near the edge of the patio. Ink black hair swept his shoulders, and his tank top left bronzed muscles exposed. He wore cut-offs and flip-flops—minimal clothing, I supposed, in case he felt the urge to dive into the nearest water.

Sunny saw him and played "Up a Lazy River."

"Yeah," River Rat breathed.

The girls tittered.

Sunny stopped singing long enough to turn over the steaks. When he cradled the guitar again and sang "Cool Clear Water," Ranger looked downright jealous.

I wondered where the rest of the cowboys were. The Tensels appeared, with George looking tuckered out and Selma appearing flustered. I wondered how long they'd last at the BVSBar Ranch. Sunny sensed their desire to be elsewhere and launched into Willie Nelson's "On the Road Again."

The man had a sense of humor.

By the time the steaks were done and we'd lined up to serve our plates, the sun had nearly set.

I didn't see Bertha anywhere. She apparently thought Vicki could handle the rest of the evening.

The only light came from candles on tables and soft lights glowing from corners of the patio. Sam smiled at me. I wished I could go to sleep in his arms listening to Sunny Barlow sing.

Sunny looked toward the back of the patio and frowned. I craned around to see Wayne Rickoff and Monty stroll in late to the barbecue. Maybe they'd been trying to fix the skeet trap machine. Sunny studied Rickoff with a dark scowl. Rickoff didn't seem to notice. He and Monty ambled to the grill, collected their food and returned to the back of the patio.

I heard the girls talking about why Sunny wore makeup.

"Maybe he's afraid some girl he ditched will show up and recognize him." Jangles giggled. "I'd love to discuss his history with him while I remove his makeup, flake by flake."

Vicki put marshmallows, chocolate bars and graham crackers on a fireside table. Everybody swarmed around her to make s'mores and carry the treasures to their tables.

Vicki slipped off the patio into the darkness. I guess she figured she'd done her job. Somebody else would clean up.

Rickoff finished eating and left. Monty and Ranger Travis left a few minutes later. Everybody Vicki'd had trouble with left shortly after she did, like an exodus of foxes scenting a rabbit. Goosebumps rippled across my shoulders.

When the Tensels left, our suitemates rose to follow. Sam, apparently oblivious to the departing guests, scarfed down another s'more. Unable to sit still another minute, I rose to leave. Meredith and I waved good night to Sunny Barlow and thanked him for the music. He said he'd stay to clean up. It was getting very dark.

As we navigated the path to our cabins, it grew even darker. Sunny must have doused the campfire. We slowed and walked carefully, adjusting our eyes to seeing by moonlight. The cicadas grew louder, as if to warn us of impending danger. An owl hooted.

I grabbed Meredith's arm. "What's that noise in the brush?"

"Some animal that feeds at night, raccoon...opossum."

"How can they see to eat anything? We can barely see three feet ahead," I said.

"It might be armadillos digging with their snouts and claws, loosening the soil to find food."

"Oh."

"They catch beetles, ants, termites, worms and caterpillars with long sticky tongues."

Meredith tended to chatter when she was nervous. She had to be as eager as I was to reach our cabin. I hadn't seen horseshoe marks on the trail, but somebody must have ridden a horse there. Selma stepped in horse poop.

"My new espadrilles!" she shrieked. "Why doesn't anybody clean up this place?"

We stopped behind Selma. Millie, who'd rolled up her jeans, bent over and squinted at something clinging to the folds. "What's that?"

Dozens of crickets had landed on Millie's pant legs. Stoney's turquoise, gleaming in the moonlight, must have attracted them. Millie's cuffed jeans gave them a secure landing site. Millie squealed, shaking one leg, then the other, trying to dislodge crickets without touching them and gyrating like a crazed voodoo dancer.

Everybody moved away from her except Selma, who was occupied with scraping horse poop off her shoes. Since Selma was close to Millie, a few crickets jumped toward her. When both women screamed with terror, we all closed in and started flipping critters off them.

Sunny Barlow walked up. "What's going on?"

"Crickets." Jangles smiled. "We're getting rid of them." She and Stoney flicked crickets like pros.

As soon as Selma was mostly cricket-free, she marched ahead toward their cabin, fuming. George seemed happy to let her go. He meandered around until I lost sight of him in the darkness.

"Guess I'll turn in," Sunny said. He was carrying an ice chest.

Meredith whispered. "He's so good looking. What's the ice chest—?"

He heard her. "I keep clown makeup in it," he said, "so it won't melt. Got more ice from the kitchen."

He detoured toward his cabin.

"Good idea," I said, turning to Meredith. "We should put our makeup in that cooler I brought."

Sam looked at me like I was crazy. He muttered under his breath. "The guy probably hides sharp knives in that cooler... ex-con serial killer protecting his identity. Hates city people. Knows they flock to dude ranches. Comes here to kill them."

I thought he was teasing, but I couldn't see his face. I was glad Millie didn't hear him.

We heard a loud boom. Everybody froze. "Was that thunder?" I said. "A shot?"

Sam slipped his hand under his shirt. "Maybe Rickoff practices in the dark."

Jangles gave him a disgusted look. "Come on, girls. It's time we got back to our cabin."

"Good idea," Sam said. "Loud noises attract snakes."

Millie screeched, grabbed the others and they bolted for their cabin.

"You're impossible," I said to Sam.

"Yeah." He chuckled. "It's time everybody got to bed anyway." He swaggered toward his cabin. "We should've brought a flashlight."

Meredith and I were relieved to get to our bungalow and slip inside. "What do you think that boom was?" I asked her.

"Sounded like a shot. Maybe somebody shot a rabbit or a javelina."

"Probably. I'm too tired to care."

"Me, too."

"I'll check my mail." I powered up my laptop and found a timely letter.

Dear Aggie,

My husband says I'm a good camper. I can set up tents and cook with minimal utensils. I've learned to hike in khaki clothes that resemble Burka gear to protect my skin without suffocating. Despite beautiful scenery, I walk eyes-to-the-ground to avoid stepping on some creature. But at night, I get nervous. Unfamiliar noises scare me. Can you help?

Nervous Nelly

Dear Nervous Nelly,

When we escape our canned-air habitats after dark, we discover that some creatures prefer nighttime to daytime. Armadillos, bats, hedgehogs, raccoons and opossums forage through brush looking for something to eat. They are totally uninterested in you.

Wolves howl mournfully, coyotes sound like Chihuahuas barking, and hedgehogs are into heavy breathing. With their looks, go figure.

Crickets' legs rubbing together sound like tiny nail files doing battle. Whippoorwills sound like they're whistling at girls, and owls hoot like disapproving grandmothers.
I don't recommend hiking at night, but the most likely danger is stepping in critter poop. Why not sit inside in a comfy chair with your feet up? Open your window, leave the screen on and try to identify what's making the sounds.

Pleasantly perched night owl,
Aggie

It was comforting writing about nocturnal creatures. People were scary. I kept thinking about that boom. Why would somebody be shooting in the dark? I remembered how Sunny had glared at

Rickoff, and how Rickoff, Ranger and Monty had slipped away right after Vicki left, as if they were tracking her.

What did Sunny have in that ice chest? What was he hiding behind that makeup?

Ten

Meredith fell into her bunk and didn't move. After the evening's turmoil, I longed to sleep soundly.

Stoney's voice carried through the bathroom. "It's too dang hot in here. This air conditioning's lousy. Let's get these windows up. At least we'll be able to breathe."

Once she'd shoved up every sash, we had a few minutes' peace. Then Millie spoke in a stage whisper. "What are those noises outside?"

"Normal night sounds, Millie," Stoney said. "Birds, crickets, whatever. Go to sleep."

"What if they get in?"

"They'll never make it to you. You're too high off the floor."

"Will you two pipe down," Jangles said. "I'm having enough trouble figuring out which parts to hang over the side of this bunk so the rest of me will stay in."

They finally settled down. I thought we might actually get some sleep until I heard the second boom.

"Hear that shot?" Jangles shouted.

"Was it thunder?" Millie asked.

"It was a shot. You hear a shot when you're in the brush trying to hide because you're doing your business," Jangles said, "and you never forget the sound."

"For Pete's sake. Who'd be shooting at night?" Stoney said. "A car could have backfired. It was probably only thunder. The rain will cool us off. Can we please get some sleep?"

Meredith had the pillow over her head and didn't stir. I thought about how isolated we were. It seemed as though I'd always been isolated. When my parents died, I'd been uprooted to Uncle Charlie and Aunt Novena's farm. When I graduated high school, I had to leave their farm to find work in Chicago. Then I fell for Lester, and he left. That's when I had to leave my friends Katy and Sam Vanderhoven to go work at the branch bank in the suburbs. When Sam's family died, he was too full of grief to want to see anybody. I was alone again.

When I moved to Texas to start over, met Meredith and saw Sam again, it had been over two years since he'd lost his family. He said he couldn't stand Chicago's winters. I knew he was escaping memories, not the weather.

Now that Sam and Meredith were both here in Texas, I knew I'd never leave. I never wanted to be alone again.

I finally drifted into a restless sleep. In my dream, Wayne Rickoff was aiming at targets. Sam, Meredith, Vicki, Sunny and a huge snake were pinned to five bull's eyes. When Rickoff pulled the trigger, the targets blew up.

The view morphed into a river scene. Meredith, Sam, Vicki and I paddled around in canoes, heading straight for a whirlpool. River Rat cackled insanely from the riverbank. As I slipped into the whirlpool, my mind emptied and I relaxed.

My short night ended with a loud thump. I was surprised to hear Millie cursing like a sailor. She must have sat up too quickly and cracked her head on the ceiling. The other two fussed at her for waking them up. After all that ruckus, I was thoroughly awake. Millie apparently hadn't knocked herself out, or else I'd hear Jangles and Stoney calling for help to revive her.

Through the window, I saw streaks trying to light the sky. I rose and staggered around the cabin, trying to find my clothes and dress without waking Meredith.

When I stepped outside, dawn barely lit the porch. I inhaled the vanilla scent of summer phlox. No wonder people loved the Hill Country. The air alone could probably cure most ailments.

Birds sang to the new morning. I heard the buzzy notes of a golden-cheeked warbler. Not far off the path, in a circle of stunted junipers, two warblers preened and sang. I looked up just as hesitant light began to illuminate high clouds floating in the blue sky. What a perfect time to enjoy a solitary walk to the lodge.

When I reached the building, I eased up the front porch steps and slid into a rocker. Bertha might not be awake, or at least not ready for company.

I had leaned my head back against the rocker when I heard a scream inside the lodge.

Eleven

I sprang up, yanked open the lodge door and charged into the dining hall. The cries came from the kitchen. When I blasted through the swinging doors, Maria, the cook, shrieked as she stared into the open horizontal freezer. I zoomed to her side and looked down. Bertha closed in behind me, puffing hard. Across the top of the freezer contents lay a stiff snake. A tiny piece of wire protruded from its scaly mouth.

Bertha put her hands on her hips. "Somebody's got a weird sense of humor, Maria. This snake ain't goin' nowhere. It's dang near frozen. It'll be a stick in an hour. I'll throw it out later. Help me get breakfast ready." She slammed the freezer door shut.

Maria whimpered, her eyes huge.

Her pulse was probably sprinting faster than mine. She stumbled in the general direction of the sink. I hoped she didn't need anything else from the freezer. Bertha's tone meant Maria should work on breakfast, snake or no snake.

I made my way back to the dining room, took eight or ten deep breaths and plopped myself on a chair.

Meredith bounced in the front door, followed by Sam wearing jeans and a khaki shirt—the same type shirt he wore with outlandish ties at SAPD. His shirttail hung out.

I longed to run to him, have him hold me and rest my cheek against the chest hair peeking out above his shirt button. As he dragged his boots across the floor, I remembered the wranglers had scheduled him and George Tensel for a morning horseback ride.

"Tensel snored like an elephant last night," Sam said. "I could hear him through the bathroom. Selma bitched at him, but he never even woke up." He studied my face. "You look a little pale."

"Not enough sleep." I turned to Meredith, "I was amazed you slept through the racket in cabin six. Jangles thought she heard a shot. The sound woke me, but I wasn't sure what it was. Maybe a car backfired."

Sam's scrunched his eyebrows. "Why would anybody be driving around eighteen hundred acres at night?"

"Maybe somebody was shooting rabbits," I said. I was too sleep-deprived to discuss possibilities.

"If Rickoff shoots in the dark, he's even crazier than he looks."

I didn't tell them about the snake in the freezer. Why ruin Meredith's breakfast? I wanted to ponder why somebody'd dump a snake in there. Why play a cruel joke on Maria?

After everybody conquered the breakfast buffet, the Tensels left their table and joined us at ours.

"I can't believe I'm going to climb on a horse," George said. "I haven't ridden on anything but a car seat in forty years."

"We know that, George," Selma said.

"I'm looking forward to gauchoing through the countryside," Sam said, winking at me. He was clearly beginning to enjoy himself. The smile on his face made me wonder if he was considering springing a surprise on George during the trail ride.

Twelve

When the men headed for the stables, Selma, Meredith and I returned to our cabins to put on swimsuits. Meredith and I wore tank suits and flip-flops. We thought we looked outdoorsy and ready for a dip in the river. Selma strolled up to join us in a high-cut suit with shorts over it. Both garments bulged. I'd eat smaller portions at tonight's campfire.

The cabin six girls had apparently gone ahead. We three trod to the waterfront.

"Texas is home to a wider diversity of snakes and lizards than any other state in the nation," Meredith said. "Think we should tell Millie?"

"Only if you want to see her run full tilt to her car," I said.

"I might follow her," Selma said.

"Actually, lizards aren't venomous. Neither are most snakes. They're deadly to prey, but not to humans," Meredith said. "Only a couple of types are venomous to humans—pit vipers and coral snakes like the one..."

"Don't remind us. Not if you want us to get in that river," I said. "Don't people swim in the Guadalupe and Medina Rivers all the time?"

"Exactly. Snakes avoid people."

When we reached the waterfront, we saw a Navy SEAL outfitted in full-body diving gear.

We realized it was Millie.

She announced she wasn't about to touch anything slimy.

Meredith whispered to me, "Think I should tell her if she sees a snake floating at rest, she should avoid it?"

"Don't think I'd mention it."

Stoney wore a competition tank suit. She had tied a warm-up top around her hips and wore obsolete tennis shoes.

Jangles had covered her swimsuit with a striped tent dress. Her frock spread out over the dock like a porch umbrella. Rehabilitated rhinestones sparkling from her sandals peeked out from underneath her tent. She awaited River Rat's instructions.

River Rat smiled seductively. "Let's get you tadpoles and fish in the water and see how you swim. You first, Millie. Put on these swim fins." He must have feared she'd sink, encased in so much rubber. He led the shivering creature down a gentle embankment and glided her into the water, talking softly in her ear while he held her hand.

Millie had a death grip on River Rat's arm. He called to Jangles. "You're next, Jangles. Come on in." She threw off her tent and waddled into the shallows, a broad smile on her face.

"Good, good," said Rat. "That's it. Get a little deeper. Up to your chest. Good. You're going to float just fine, Jangles. Ready, Stoney?"

Stoney yanked off her warm-up, kicked off her tennis shoes, flung her towel at the discard pile and plunged off the dock.

"Good thing you did a flat dive," Rat said. "It's pretty shallow there."

Stoney beamed and plowed through the water like a plumber's snake.

"Go ahead, Selma." Rat called.

Selma slipped in cautiously and paddled around, keeping one eye on the bank.

Rat watched them navigate for a while, then nodded for Meredith and me to get in. We put on life jackets, slid in and swam around. The water was cold. Shaded by oaks and cypress trees, this part of the Medina River wouldn't warm up until the sun reached full potential later in the day.

"You're okay in the water," Rat said to Meredith and me. "Why don't you get out and drag a canoe to the water's edge."

We crawled up the bank and walked over to study three canoes and three kayaks lined up perpendicular to the shoreline. We selected a canoe and tugged it toward the water. Rat told Meredith to steady the craft sideways to shore while I climbed in and perched on the front seat. He told me to use my oar to hug our boat close to the bank while Meredith slid onto the back seat.

"Aggie," Rat said, "you're the paddler who determines the direction of the craft. To do that, you paddle your oar on one side, then the other to guide the canoe."

Meredith sat still with her oar across her lap. "Your job," Rat told her, "is to steady the craft. Instead of paddling, you place your oar upright in the water on alternate sides, turning it like a rudder to steady the canoe as it glides along."

His instructions were clear, and we started moving. Mostly forward. We laughed at our ineptitude but learned how to maneuver. Jangles swam over to join our fun and looped her elbows over the side of the canoe.

"You make it look easy," she said.

"Hey, don't..."

"Uh-oh..."

We knew we were capsizing.

We dove in on either side of Jangles, pushing our feet against the canoe. Fortunately, the canoe didn't hit Jangles when it flipped. We bobbed around and found oars while Jangles sputtered apologies.

"Everybody swim to the bank and climb out," Rat bellowed. His dark eyes flashed. "I'll get the friggin' canoe."

It floated like a slice of upturned cantaloupe. Rat had to swim to the bank with Millie, convince her to let go of his hand and push her up on solid ground. Then he could deal with the boat. He plunged back in and righted the canoe. By that time, everybody had crawled back up on the bank. Meredith and I sat quietly, feeling foolish and knowing that Jangles felt worse.

I concentrated on squeezing water from my hair until the backs of my legs started to burn. I jumped up screeching and danced around rubbing the backs of my thighs. My legs were on fire from hips to ankles. “Something stings!”

“You must have sat in poison ivy,” Rat said. “Don’t rub it. Get back in the water.”

I held my nose and jumped in.

Meredith pointed at the culprit. “See that green ivy-like plant with three leaflets? That’s poison ivy, all right.”

At least some creature hadn’t stung me. I treaded water and let cool water ease the burning. Maybe I could just stay in the river until class ended.

“You’ll have to walk to the lodge,” Rat said. “Bertha has first aid remedies. We’ll be along shortly. Come on, everybody. Back in the water.”

I found Rat somewhat lacking in sympathy. Maybe he’d been given instructions never to let his river class end prematurely. Perhaps marijuana time came after class.

“I’ll come with you,” Meredith said.

I waved her off. “Enjoy the river. I’ll be fine.”

Thirteen

I scurried up the bank, slid into flip-flips and scooted toward the lodge as fast as I could with my beet-red thighs stinging as if they were on fire. I was dying to scratch. The sensation was worse than when curiosity made my feet itch.

Bertha's yellow Jeep was parked by the lodge. An unfamiliar car was parked alongside. I heard angry voices inside the lodge—an increasingly regular event at the BVSBar Ranch.

A man bellowed, "Maybe you sped up the dehydration. What'd you put in those thermoses?"

"I didn't put anything in their thermoses." Bertha yelled back. "And I'll never sell you this ranch. You never cared one whit about it."

I hated to interrupt, but I couldn't stand still much longer and eavesdrop with my backside burning. Clearing my throat, I charged through the door.

"Bertha, I'm sorry to intrude, but I sat in poison ivy. River Rat said you had remedies."

"Come to my room. I'll fix you up." She flipped her wrist toward the couple. "This is Herb and Bitsy Vernon. Herb's my cousin. His parents owned the BVSBar."

Herb, who looked about Bertha's age, muttered something that sounded like, "Still should."

Bitsy, much younger than Herb, smiled from under her bleached Barbie Doll helmet.

I nodded at them and whipped into Bertha's room.

Bertha slammed the door. "Go into the bathroom, get your swimsuit off and stand in the tub with your rear facing the faucets."

My face probably turned as red as the backs of my thighs, but I didn't have much choice. She opened a huge medicine chest and whipped a gallon bottle of rubbing alcohol off a shelf.

I recognized a bottle of diet pills and diuretics. The other labels weren't familiar.

"I'm going to pour this on the backs of your legs and rinse you with cool water. We can't rub it on. Rubbing spreads the oils that are makin' you itch."

She poured alcohol on me and rinsed me with cool water. I felt relief from the stinging but shivered from the cold. She gave me a towel to wrap my upper body.

"Don't get that towel near the poison ivy area. You'll spread the toxin around."

I promised I wouldn't. Standing naked in her bathtub with my legs stinging, I'd have promised just about anything.

"Do Herb and Bitsy come here often?" My teeth chattered.

"He hates the place. Always has. Just shows up when he needs money. I sure don't have any extra to give him. He wants some oil company to drill on the ranch so he'll get royalties."

"But it's your ranch, isn't it?"

"Sure is. Herb and I each own half the minerals, but I own executive rights. I decide who can drill. Nobody's going to bring in a bunch of trucks and drilling rigs and make a mess of this gorgeous piece of land."

"You wouldn't have to work so hard...keep operating the place as a guest ranch and watch over Angora goats and cows like you do..."

She sloshed me with alcohol. "That's what they say. But instead of this beautiful ranch, I'd have a job site with nuthin' but a bunch of roads and trucks and land full of holes." She doused me with colder water.

My goose bumps might become permanent. My skin would look like cottage cheese.

"Besides," she said, "most oil fields are drilled south of the Hill Country." She stared at me. "How'd you know we have Angora goats?"

"I read about the ranch before we came. I heard your aunt and uncle died on this ranch and you found them." My teeth were still chattering. "That must have been awful."

She drenched me with alcohol and water twice before she answered. My whole body quivered from the cold.

"It was awful," she said. "And that little snot"—she gestured toward the closed door—"thinks I..." She wheeled around to the medicine cabinet so fast, I twitched. When she opened the cabinet again, I saw more pill bottles: vitamins, diuretics, blood pressure medicine, plus other unfamiliar drugs. She grabbed another jug. When she closed the cabinet door, I noticed papers on top of the adjacent cabinet and saw the words "drilling...well...Bandera County." Some oil company had approached Bertha.

When she turned back toward me, her face was dark as a rain cloud. "Turn around," she said.

I turned slowly. What was she going to do? The hair on my neck stood up. When she squirted something cold on my legs, I almost jumped out of my towel.

"That's calamine lotion. After you shower, get somebody to drip it on you." From the corner of my eye, I saw her reach toward me. I whipped around. She handed me the jug of lotion.

"I'm going to give you this bottle of Clorox mixed with water." She handed me the other gallon jug. "When you think you can't stand any more itching, get in the shower and pour this Clorox over your legs. Rinse with cool water. Warm water spreads the poison ivy oil."

There was no way I could wrench on my swimsuit without touching my legs.

Bertha loaned me a pink, over-the-head housedress splotched with gigantic purple flowers.

I'd have to walk back to my cabin wearing this obnoxious muumuu and lugging two jugs. I'd probably bump into Sam. To lighten my dour thoughts, I pictured River Rat's face with Millie clutching his hand the whole time I was gone.

I donned the muumuu, slipped past the Vernons, muttered "Pleased to meet you" and stepped onto the front porch. I eased toward the left side of the lodge, put down the jugs and flattened myself against the side of the building, trying to hide in my purple flowers. As long as I wasn't itching, I might as well stick around to hear what the Vernons and Bertha said to each other. They talked loudly.

"Don't you ever check the place where they drilled?" Herb barked. "I remember when I was a kid seeing a bunch of trucks and that tall drilling rig out there somewhere. It was so dang hot and dry, there wasn't much else to do besides watch guys drive around and struggle with equipment. When I'd come to the house, all Mom and Dad talked about was how long the drought was going to last—how they couldn't make a living on this sorry piece of land. When they sent me to school in San Antonio, I was plenty ready to leave this wilderness. You need to find that well, Bertha. Might not be dry anymore. Might be oil all over the damn place."

"Forget it, Herb. That was over five years ago. Nothin's gushin' out there. The whole area's probably covered over with mesquite by now. Nobody's gonna' drill on the BVSBar. You want to try to find some dry hole? Go search. Then get off my ranch and leave me in peace."

There was certainly no love lost between Bertha and cousin Herb. If an oil company drilled and came up with a dry hole, they must have abandoned the well, like Bertha said. Was the abandoned well the 'treasure' the Vernons sought five years earlier when they perished? In five years, the area probably had grown over. But it wouldn't have been covered over when the Vernons went there. What drew them to that well? What happened there to cause their deaths? I wondered if there was some way to locate the original drilling site.

Herb was cursing. He and Bertha exchanged a few more gruff remarks, but I couldn't make out what they said. When Herb shoved Bitsy through the door and let it slam back against the wall, I had to slide farther back down the side of the lodge and flatten myself against the stone so my purple flowers wouldn't give me away. At least the limestone felt cool and the backs of my legs weren't stinging.

Herb and Bitsy stomped down the steps to their car. Herb turned, looked back at the building and spotted me. He snapped at Bitsy. "Get in the car."

Fourteen

I cringed against the building, but I knew Herb Vernon had seen my flowers. I picked up my jugs and walked toward him with a smile on my face. "I thought I'd walk to the river, but these jugs are awfully heavy."

Frowning, he stopped three feet in front of me. "Kind of a strange time to be taking a stroll, don't you think? Suffering with poison ivy? Carrying two jugs?"

"You're right. I'll take the main path to our cabin, like always." I attempted to walk around him. He moved left and blocked me. I sensed rage building inside him.

"Were you eavesdropping?" he asked.

I shook my head. "Why would I do that?"

He glowered. "I don't know. Why would you? How long have you known Bertha?"

"Just since we got here on Thursday." I rounded my eyes and tried my best to appear angelic. "She's a nice lady."

"That's debatable. You better get back to your cabin and treat your wilderness rash with that...whatever it is."

"You're right. So nice to meet y'all."

"Yeah."

When I hurried down the path, I could feel him staring at my back, as though he'd launched a searing arrow. I finally heard their car start.

After I turned to watch their vehicle pull away, I walked even faster down the path to our cabin. It was almost lunch time, so everybody would be returning from morning activities, and I looked like a Medicare matron in her lousiest housedress.

Sure enough, my friends sauntered up from the river path accompanied by Sam and George. I longed to turn heel and race to the cabin, but I was trapped.

"Let's see what Bertha gave you," Meredith said. She studied the labels. "I've read about these. They're supposed to work. Do they help?"

I nodded.

"Are you sure you won't have to be hospitalized?" Millie asked. "I heard of a teacher who chewed poison ivy leaves for years to show off for his students. He ended up in the hospital."

I looked at Meredith.

"It could happen after multiple exposures," she said. "This is your first exposure, right?"

I nodded.

"You'll be okay."

"I heard about one woman," Stoney said, "who was exposed to the sap every year while she washed her husband's hunting clothes. After several years, she had a severe reaction. Her kidneys shut down, and she died."

I probably aged ten years from sitting in poison ivy, sharing Bertha's wardrobe and dealing with Herb. Now I had to worry about dying.

"Too bad her husband didn't wash his own hunting clothes," Selma said, leering at George.

"I read about that woman," Meredith said. "She developed a tremendous sensitivity. It was a very unusual case."

Sam studied my purple flowers. "Nice dress."

I glared at him. He knew better than to laugh. George told me not to go near the horses. He said I might scare them.

Sam scowled at him, which made me feel better than Bertha's remedies.

"Let's all get to our cabins," he told the Tensels. When we arrived at our cabin, Jangles offered to lend me a tent dress. I smiled at her.

"I packed a loose sundress that billows away from my legs. I think it'll work. Thanks."

While Meredith and the girls showered off river water, I put a non-itchy towel on the chair by the table, sat with my rear end barely touching, and typed "Obituary: Max and Billy Sue Vernon" into WebCrawler. I read:

"Long-time Bandera County residents and owners of the BVSBar Ranch, Max and Billy Sue Vernon, were found dead on their ranch Thursday, July 30, 1992, from apparent dehydration and heat stroke. They were 59 years old and had been high school sweethearts. Max named the ranch after Billy Sue, with V, for Vernon, as the middle initial. Much beloved by family and friends, they contributed greatly to Bandera and the surrounding area. They were predeceased by Mrs. Vernon's brother and his wife, Roger and Beatrice Sampson. Survivors include the Vernons' son, Herbert Vernon, their niece, Bertha Sampson, and many Hill Country friends. Visitation will be at Grimes Funeral Home, on Sunday, August 2, from 6:00 to 8:00 p.m. A service for the Vernons will be held at First Baptist Church on Monday, August 3 at 2:00 p.m."

How could I learn more about the Vernons' untimely deaths? With Herb and Bertha being the couple's only survivors, there were no other relatives Sam and I could question about circumstances surrounding their untimely demise. I didn't expect the Grimes Funeral Home to discuss the tragic deaths of Bandera's beloved residents with outsiders. I wondered if I could talk Sam into getting a copy of the couples' autopsy reports.

I researched Bertha and cousin Herb: they were the same age, forty-four. They would have been thirty-nine when Max and Billy Sue died. The Vernons had Herb in 1953, a year or two into the historical drought that began in Texas and the southwest and lasted until the mid-1960s.

Herb's overriding childhood memory must have been the effect of the drought on his family and this land. They couldn't farm. They survived by converting marginal farm and ranch land into a dude ranch.

Despite conflicts at the ranch, I still had a column to write, so I needed to check my mail. There was only one letter, but it made me think.

Dear Aggie,

We lived in the northeast, spent time in Kansas and are now in Missouri. My husband got a promotion and we're moving to Texas, south of Austin. All I can think of is tumbleweeds, guns and bluster. How will I ever survive?

Worried Willa

Dear Worried,

When you drive southwest from Missouri and hit the Oklahoma line, vistas open up. At the Texas border, you begin to see broader expanses of land. When a person can see the horizon, her imagination opens like the landscape. Daydreams become possibilities.

Texans love their land and drive hard bargains to keep it. Space gives them freedom of movement and thought. They believe when people are crowded together, they're bound to get testy. Have you experienced that?

Tumbleweeds blow across West Texas deserts, but that's about four hundred miles from where you'll be in Austin. It's true many Texans grow up around guns. To people with a frontier heritage, firearms mean protection. Texans respect their deadly potential and learn to handle them safely. Doesn't always work, but most of the time it does.

Bluster is only a way of talking: big state, big dreams, big mouths. Don't let it fool you. Underneath the bluster, you'll find hearts of gold and people who'll help anybody who needs it. Just don't try to take something from a Texan before they offer.

Turning Texan,
Aggie

I thought about Texans I'd met at the ranch. How far would Bertha go to get and keep the BVSBar? How far would Herb Vernon go to reclaim it? Vicki had grown to love the Hill Country. Could she really leave?

When it was time to put on my sundress, I was careful to avoid my ivy patch. To boost my spirits, I applied extra makeup. If the calamine lotion didn't wear off and I stood up to eat, I might make it through lunch.

Sam joined Meredith and me to walk to the lodge. Before he could tell us about his morning ride, I told them about Herb and Bitsy Vernon.

"This is turning into quite a vacation spot," Sam said.

We walked in silence, immersed in thought. If I could figure out who killed the Vernons, Sam could relax and enjoy a much-needed vacation. He might finally realize I had sound sleuthing skills. I had to deduce who put a snake in the freezer.

Before we reached the lodge, Meredith stopped.

"Do you think Bertha is capable of killing her own aunt and uncle to get this ranch?"

Fifteen

Thinking about the value of the ranch, I studied the dining hall. The decorating theme was dead animals. Heads of deer, bison, and elk were mounted on wall plaques near the ceiling. How could anybody shoot the elegant creatures, especially deer and elk, unless they needed to consume the meat to survive? Didn't elk live in colder climates anyway? What was an elk's head doing up there?

A bison's dull eyes stared across the dining room. Bison didn't roam free anymore except in national parks, nature preserves or private commercial herds. Somebody had special access to kill that bison.

Something about the bison's face reminded me of Dr. Carmody, my Aspects of Aging professor from last Semester at University of the Holy Trinity. Maybe it was the bison's eyes: dull, yet cunning. To force my mind off the professor, I studied the ceiling.

Fish and bobcats hung at raucous angles from ceiling wires, which made them appear to be sizing up guests. I was intrigued by two bobcats. One was larger than the other, probably a male and female. Their ears were tipped with black tufts, which supposedly collected sound to sharpen their hearing. I'd read they had excellent eyesight for day and night vision and were abundant in South Texas.

Light fur cascading down their cheeks made them look loveable. I wanted to touch it to see if was soft. Bobcats were supposed to be secretive, shy, and solitary, but some were rambunctious and overly curious. Like me. Maybe that's why those two ended up hanging from the ceiling.

Wire served multiple other purposes on a ranch: stringing fences, tying hay bales and hanging farm implements. Ranger Travis used it to sculpt animals and birds, but I was mystified by the wire protruding from the mouth of the snake we found in the freezer.

The cabin six girls and Selma entered the dining hall with their hair still damp. Jangles' upswept wet hair looked like the stem on a pumpkin. Stoney appeared particularly boyish with her hair slicked back. Millie looked like a damp rag doll. They must be starving from exercise to risk appearing in public with wet hair.

Selma had probably tried to fluff her hair while she argued with George over who had endured the lousiest morning. Conflict must have made her hungry. She beat George to the buffet line. I saw her and Bertha glare jealously at Vicki's dry, fluffy locks.

Wranglers Ranger and Monty moseyed in, followed by River Rat, whose blow-dried hair hung shiny and straight to his shoulders. He winked at his aquatic gang of tadpoles, frogs and fish.

I motioned George to go ahead—he walked with widespread legs—so he could catch up with Selma. After they filled their plates, they went to sit by Wayne Rickoff. He was probably the only member of the staff they didn't currently associate with suffering.

I slipped into the buffet line with Meredith and Sam, wishing I could nibble standing up. After we selected our food, I suggested we choose a table near Rickoff and the Tensels. I wanted to eavesdrop.

Picking bites of food off my plate, I sat on one hipbone within earshot of their table, wondering how many ceiling creatures Rickoff had killed. He started bragging in a loud voice about his hunting prowess.

"I had this friend who worked at a high fence game ranch in Wisconsin that had trophy white-tail deer and elk," Rickoff said. "'Course it's illegal to shoot elk. He said we ought to go hunting in the Northwoods in the Chequamegon and Nicolet National Forest."

Rickoff's buddy couldn't risk his job at the game ranch, but he was ready to hunt illegally with Rickoff in a national forest.

Meredith leaned over and whispered in my ear, "There's a Sandhill Wildlife Area in the center of Wisconsin where the state manages a herd of bison. Do you suppose Rickoff managed to go there and kill that bison?"

I was appalled and even more intent on listening. "I got me a .338 Winchester magnum with 250-grain bullets," Rickoff said.

His weapon sounded huge, like a Bazooka. George Tensel looked interested. "I guess those big elk are easy to see, right?"

"Not really. They hang out in thick dark timber where trees have burned or blown down in a storm. We found a big blow-down area where trees were a tangled mess. A second growth had come up. Elk were amazingly hard to see in there. It's hard to tell 'em from deer." He winked at George. "But we saw big tracks and droppings."

Selma's face registered disgust.

"We found an area where elk had scratched hides and horns against trees, and we put up portable stands in that area. I climbed in my stand expecting a long wait and adjusted my Leopold scope to make sure I could see in the dark."

Vicki apparently overheard Wayne Rickoff and appeared to be repelled at the thought of his killing elegant animals in her home state.

She told people around her she needed to ride her horse and left.

Rickoff carried on. "Not ten minutes after I got in the stand, I caught movement of a big animal comin' through tangled trees. It was amazing to see how easily he got around in there. It was a small buck headed right for my blind. I raised my rifle. He got almost within range and then bolted off. I thought he winded me. Then a bigger buck came in from the right. This was the animal I came looking for. He turned broadside. I sighted him just as he whirled and took off. When I shot, his rear was to me."

Sam squirmed in his seat and passed his hand over the area where I guessed he'd hidden the Glock.

"He bled a lot," Rickoff said, "but I tracked him. When I finally caught up to him, he'd almost bled out. That's when I saw that huge rack. I had me a trophy elk. That's him...up there." He gestured to the elk head on the wall.

Rickoff apparently didn't care where or how he shot animals and wasn't too keen on people. Millie must have been listening. Her face turned green, and she stumbled out of the dining hall.

Sam might be right. We should leave this ranch. Sunny, the last to fill his plate, walked over to join us. His makeup was thinner than usual. He chatted and smiled at Meredith. With his classic features and smooth skin, I thought he would be extraordinarily handsome without that makeup. For a second, window light caught his face from an angle and highlighted a scar that ran from his ear all the way down his jaw and faded into his neck. So that was what he wanted to hide.

"You look uncomfortable," he said, noticing the awkward way I was sitting.

"Had a little encounter with poison ivy." I sipped tea from my glass. "I'd rather be standing up."

Bertha whacked her glass with a spoon. "We don't have planned activities this afternoon. If you want to practice what you learned, tell your instructors, and they'll meet you at the site. Cabin air conditioners aren't working. If you want to rest on your bunks, I've got small fans you can use 'til the weather breaks."

The girls glanced at each other. Should they bask in Rat's charm by the river in the heat of the day or try to rest in a steamy cabin? I decided a fan would feel good blowing on my poison ivy patch and lined up to get one from Bertha.

When I approached, she said, "I made jewelweed ice cubes. If you rub them on, it'll relieve the stinging. Jewelweed's pretty rare around here, but I make tea with what I can find and freeze it into cubes. Go get a package of 'em from the kitchen freezer—orange-colored cubes in one-quart freezer bags."

I hesitated.

“Don’t worry,” she said. “The freezer’s been cleaned out. Go back for more cubes later if you need ’em. Here’s your fan.”

Sixteen

Reluctantly, I went to the kitchen and slowly pried up the freezer lid. Maria, washing dishes, turned around and followed my progress with wide eyes. I scoured the recesses of the freezer box. The snake was gone. I picked up a bag of cubes and held them up for her.

"Mira? Recogí una bolsa de cubos. Son buenos para Zumaque." I told her I'd retrieved a bag of cubes that were good for treating poison ivy. She raised her eyebrows, surprised and delighted I spoke Spanish, and dried her hands on a towel.

"Señora Bertha told me to get the ice cubes," I continued in Spanish. "The snake is gone." I made a slithering motion with my hands and gestured that the reptile was far away.

"Gracias a Dios." She crossed herself.

"Yes, gracias a Dios." I wondered what Maria remembered about the Vernons' deaths. She appeared to be in her sixties and had probably worked for the Vernon family for many years. I put the bag of cubes back in the freezer and sat at the kitchen table. "I heard Bertha was the one who found her aunt and uncle when they died here on the ranch," I said in Spanish.

"That's right," she said. "Poor woman."

"I heard they were going on some kind of treasure hunt."

"I don't know anything about that. They said they were going to check the site where they drilled the old well. They would drive part way and then walk. Mrs. Vernon liked to exercise to stay thin."

"Did they take water?"

"Oh, yes. Señor Max drank a lot of water. They took thermoses. I made them sandwiches, too." She frowned. "It was strange they had trouble. Two days earlier, they spent the whole day wandering over the ranch without any problems. The day after that, they went to San Antonio to attend to business and returned to the ranch late in the afternoon. Their son Herb came here that evening, stayed overnight and left early the next morning. That was the day the Vernons decided to drive over the ranch again." She blinked back tears. "They never came back." She pulled up her apron to wipe her eyes.

"You knew them a long time?"

"I came to the ranch before they married. We three helped Señor Vernon's father build this ranch. When there was no rain, we worked together to save it. I helped raise Herb. When Ms. Bertha was orphaned and came here, she helped me cook while I taught her about the ranch."

"I guess Bertha and Herb were devastated when the Vernons died?"

"Oh, yes. They shed many tears."

"After Herb grew up, while the Vernons were still alive, did Herb come back to the ranch very often?"

"No. He never really liked the ranch. When he was twelve, his parents sent him to school in San Antonio. He was happy to go. He'd come home for holidays...vacations. After he grew up, I think he only came when he needed money." She hung her head, embarrassed.

"Didn't he have a job?"

"After he quit going to school, I think he had lots of jobs. But they didn't seem to last long."

"Do you know why he came here the night before the Vernons died? Did he need money?"

"I don't know, Señora."

I expressed my condolences for the Vernons' deaths.

Maria had been part of the family. To cheer her up, I told her how much everybody enjoyed the good food she prepared and that I hoped to talk with her again later. Right now, I had to treat my poison ivy.

With Maria standing watch, I gingerly opened the freezer, peered inside and grabbed the bagged cubes. I scurried back through the dining room and walked fast to our cabin before the ice cubes could melt.

When I entered our abode, Meredith looked up from her reading.

"Bertha makes ice cubes from jewelweed," I said. "She says they're a good treatment for poison ivy." I placed a towel in the chair in front of my computer, rubbed orange-colored cubes on the backs of my legs and put bagged cubes at the edge of the chair. Pressing my legs against the bag to hold it in place, I sat on my tailbone.

"That's an old herbal remedy," she said. "Native American Indians and herbalists used jewelweed to counter poison ivy, bruises, cuts and burns. Even now, people chop stems of the plant, boil them, strain the orange liquid and pour it into ice cube trays. I never knew if it worked." She paused. "They say jewelweed grows on the east coast down to Florida and likes moist woods. I'd think Texas would be too dry for it to grow. Wonder where Bertha gets it?"

"She didn't say."

Meredith shrugged and returned to her reading. I turned on my laptop to check my email.

The letter came from someone who hated sun and bugs but liked cowboys.

Dear Aggie,

I've never been fond of the outdoors. At night, I can see plenty of stars just looking through my window. The only critter I care about is my dog. But I met this hunky cowboy. He and his friends want to go camping. The last time they went, a girl came home covered with a red poison ivy rash. Is there any way to prevent that? Short of giving up my cowboy?

Frenzied and fearful,
Fran

Having searched Ask Jeeves for poison ivy treatments after I sat in the stuff, I felt eminently qualified to give Fran advice.

Dear Frenzied Fran,

Poison ivy has three leaves on a reddish stem. Rashes from poison ivy, oak or sumac are caused by urushiol, a substance in their sap. If you spray deodorant containing aluminum chlorohydrate on your skin and clothes before heading outdoors, it helps prevent urushiol from irritating your skin.

If you misstep, you're going to sting and itch like crazy, but you are not going to die. First, pour water on your skin. Second, pour rubbing alcohol over the area where you brushed the plant. Third, pour on, do not rub, calamine lotion on the area. Fourth, stick your clothes in the trash. Liquid made from jewelweed cuts down the allergic reaction, but it may be hard to find in the right concentration.

Are you more interested in prevention than remedies? Study photos of poison ivy, oak and sumac. Don't sit on or walk through anything that looks like that. A sure-fire way to avoid the dangers of country living is to not go ape over a cowboy in tight jeans.

Itching but wiser,
Aggie

I decided not to mention that to keep clothes away from her itching skin, she might have to wear a ridiculously huge dress that would make her appear ninety years old.

I craved a nap. The cubes had almost melted, and my thighs were happily numb from dribbling on jewelweed and sitting on bagged ice. I lay on my bunk, covered my poison ivy patch with the bag of melting cubes and directed the fan on my legs and derriere. At least my medical condition temporarily removed me from the tensions between people and hazards of ranching. I had changed my mind about leaving, though. I had too many new questions without answers.

To relax, I imagined the sound of air conditioning purring with Sunny Barlow crooning in the distance. I pictured Sam and me lounging on a cotton-ball-soft king-sized bed in a plush country cabin with a spotless oak floor.

I stopped myself from imagining what might occur on the bed. We had a pile of obstacles to overcome.

Seventeen

When squeals from the bathroom roused me, I knew the girls must be dressing for dinner. I heard the shower running and glanced over at Meredith's empty bunk. Pushing up from my damp mattress, I let the fan blow me awake. The air was muggy. Through the front window, I saw the sun sitting low in the sky. I couldn't believe I'd slept so long.

I heard the girls chattering about the prospect of arriving early for dinner in case River Rat showed up. They wanted to schedule a swimming lesson for the following morning.

When I carried my Clorox-and-water jug to the bathroom, Jangles was drifting around the breezeway in a gauzy creation. She'd swept her hair on top of her head and captured it with a rubber band. More blond curls than usual cascaded above her head like a fountain.

Millie came in wearing a blouse with billowy sleeves, a flared denim skirt and red boots. Stoney wore jeans, a soft shirt, less turquoise than usual and a bow in her hair. The Medina River had amazing restorative properties.

Meredith was trying to decide which of her clothes would be coolest. Itching like crazy, I jumped into the shower and rinsed with Clorox. When I got out, Meredith reported that my poison ivy patches were swelling. She dripped Calamine lotion on me and dried me with the fan.

I put on my billowy sundress. We were applying makeup when I noticed my cheeks and lips were beginning to swell. I had apparently touched my face with oil from the ivy.

Someone pounded on the front door. When I answered, Sam stood there alone.

"Aren't Selma and George coming?" I asked.

"George has saddle burns. Monty told him to post. When the horse trotted, he had George straighten his legs to stand, then bend to sit back in the saddle. With every bounce, George's thighs rubbed against saddle leather."

Meredith walked up behind me. "People post on English saddles to make the horse's trot more comfortable—use the horse's motion to move forward and out of the saddle slightly. Sounds like Monty had George exaggerate the movement. What a mean thing to do."

"Yeah." Sam chuckled.

As we started down the path to the lodge, I noticed Sam was limping. "Did you post too?"

"No, but my legs haven't gripped a horse in a long time. My muscles are pretty sore."

Meredith and I exchanged glances.

"We had quite a ride." He cringed with every step. "Remember when Monty told us he'd hit some guy? This time, Monty said he'd confessed to Ranger he was an ex-con. He had gotten into a gang fight and injured some kid from another gang."

"So that's what happened," I said. "I guess gang fights are pretty common."

"Yes, but the police arrived just as Monty assaulted the other kid, so Monty was the one who did time. He thinks he owes Ranger a lot for giving him another chance. He said once Ranger finds a rich ranch guest to marry, Ranger will move up to assistant manager of the BVSBar and make Monty head wrangler."

So that's why Monty fumed when Ranger flirted with Vicki. Monty was afraid Vicki would preempt Ranger's future "rich ranch guest." If Ranger's goal was to become assistant manager, what did he think Vicki would do? Disappear?

"I'm adding ex-con Monty Malone to my list of guys to watch," Sam said.

We saw distant lightning, heard thunder and picked up our pace. Sam limped faster. With the sky overcast and thunder rumbling, I thought Bertha might cancel the barbeque. As we neared the patio, we saw tables set with red and white cloths and candles flickering inside hurricane lamps. I guessed Texans were used to the futility of predicting the weather, ignored it and carried on with their plans.

Sunny had started the fire. He plopped his boot on a table bench and cradled his guitar. The girls had claimed the table in front of him. We took a table off to one side. I was becoming an expert at sitting on my tail bone to keep my thighs off the bench. Vicki sat a couple of tables away and watched Sunny as he began to croon.

As dusk grew deeper, George and Selma straggled to the patio and sat alone. George straddled the bench sideways and stretched out his legs. I didn't see River Rat anywhere.

Wayne Rickoff and Monty Malone ambled in late and stood at the end of the patio farthest from the camp fire. I was surprised to see that Rickoff had shaved off his beard. I caught Vicki staring at him. Then she rose slowly and slipped into the darkness.

Not long after she left, Rickoff disappeared. He was so unpredictable—firing into the air when he saw a snake, aiming at people for no reason. I hoped he wasn't following Vicki.

Everybody else lined up at the barbecue grill for spare ribs, potato salad and beans. Unease made me aware of everybody's whereabouts. Once Bertha finished eating, she left. I hoped she was checking on Vicki. George Tensel lumbered off in the same general direction, and Selma followed.

Sunny played two more songs. Sam grabbed my hand under the table and made my arm tingle.

"I'm glad I came," he said.

The candle lights looked brighter. I was foolish to be tense just because people left after dinner.

When Sunny stopped singing to make s'mores, Sam dropped my hand and made a beeline for dessert. I saw lightning crackle in the distance and felt a slight breeze. We should leave before it started pouring.

Monty announced he might as well go home and sauntered off. Ranger Travis and Jangles left together. I was glad Bertha wasn't there to witness their departure. Jangles might soon acquire a wire sculpture.

Jangles' friends rose and headed for their cabin. When lightning cracked the sky, Millie started loping. Stoney yelled at her not to be a wimp while she galloped to catch up. Sam, still chewing a s'more, caught up with Meredith and me and grabbed our elbows. "Let's head for the cabins."

"May and June are Texas's rainiest months," Meredith said. "Lots of thunderstorms."

We were halfway to our cabin when we heard screams coming from the direction of the river.

Eighteen

We froze and listened—then sprinted toward the cries.

We reached the horse trail. Vicki lay on the ground unconscious. Her horse stood near her, spread-legged, with its ears pinned back, snorting as though daring anybody to approach. Its reins lay on the ground.

Selma wailed and shot furious looks at George.

He gaped at Vicki, seemingly paralyzed.

Selma's screams drew the others. Sunny rushed in and ran toward Vicki. He waved his arms at the gelding until the horse reared, whirled and galloped away. He knelt beside Vicki, touched her forehead and yelled for somebody to call 911.

Moving closer, I saw blood on Vicki's hair and on a nearby rock. Stoney and Millie ran up. Jangles and Ranger trotted up together. The bulk of her curls had escaped the rubber band and flopped like springs down the sides of her head. Her tent dress was turned quarter way around. Ranger wore most of her lipstick.

Monty loped up close behind Jangles and Ranger. When River Rat bounded up, he sank to his knees beside his sister. His hair hung forward, so I couldn't see his face. Wayne Rickoff stomped in, completing the circle, and stared down at Vicki.

Bertha pushed her way through the crowd. "Oh, my God." She fell to her knees beside Rat and Sunny, whipped a cell phone from her pocket, dialed 911 and pressed speaker phone. She laid the phone on the ground and leaned over her young assistant.

"Bandera Emergency," a voice answered.

"This is Bertha Sampson," she shouted, "at the BVSBar Ranch. We have a girl on the ground unconscious. Looks like her horse threw her. She's breathing." Bertha panted.

"What's your location on the ranch?"

"Go up the main entrance toward the lodge and cut left before you get to the building. Head for the river. There's a sign. The horse trail is by the river."

"We'll have San Antonio Air Life launch a helicopter to get the victim to the trauma center. Do you have a landing site?"

Bertha never took her eyes off Vicki. "Closest field is behind cabins three and four—southwest from where we are."

"We're dispatching EMS and the fire department. Direct the fire truck to the open field. They'll call in coordinates and prepare the landing site for Air Life. Sheriff Deputy Cranton is on the way."

Less than a half hour before, Vicki had been eating dinner on the patio. Fresh and young with her whole life ahead of her.

Within minutes, a deputy, Cranton, I presumed, pulled his car up as close as he could get to the horse trail, jumped out and came leaping toward us through the brush.

"Don't anybody move her."

We heard the EMS siren squealing up the main road. The van's headlights lit up the lodge and swung left toward us. When the van screeched to a stop, a group of EMTs loaded with gear and a stretcher bounded toward us. The fire truck pulled up behind the van.

"Get back. Get back." The emergency team swarmed Vicki. One technician put an oxygen mask on her face. Another took her vital signs. "Low pressure. Thready pulse."

Bertha scrambled toward the fire truck to give the driver directions to the landing field.

Sam, standing beside me, spoke in low tones. "Vicki doesn't look good. She might have a serious head injury."

A sob escaped me. I felt faint. He grabbed my arm to steady me. Meredith grabbed his other arm. One technician placed a cervical collar around Vicki's neck. Two others took positions behind her waist and knees and rolled her slowly on to her side, then carefully back onto the board.

"They're doing a 'log roll' to check her back for injuries," Sam said, "stabilizing and protecting her head and spine to get her ready to transport."

As they lifted her stretcher into the EMS van, I thought I heard her moan. It was the best sound I'd ever heard.

I saw Deputy Cranton don a sterile glove and pick up a blood-spattered rock from the area where Vicki fell and put it in a Zip-loc bag.

"We need information about the girl. Who knows her?" the medical technician said.

Bertha walked toward him. I slipped closer. The technician asked Bertha for Vicki's full name, parents' names and contact information and whether she knew Vicki's medical history.

Bertha repeated the names of Vicki and her parents. "I can't remember the other things," she said, "but I can fax you Vicki's employment application with medical records." The technician gave her his card.

"We'll get her as close as possible to the copter and help load her," he said.

The medical team was doing everything they could, but I was glad Vicki couldn't hear them. She'd be terrified.

"Where will they take her?" I asked Sam. I wondered if Meredith felt as woozy as I did. Hearing particulars might help me remain conscious.

"San Antonio University Hospital," Sam said. "It's the closest trauma center. The first hour after an injury is the most critical. Doctors will be evaluating her well within that time frame."

I prayed for Vicki, the young, confused girl with so many possibilities ahead. The EMS van rolled back on to the main road and headed toward the field with poor Vicki jostling inside.

We saw the helicopter in the sky and ran down the horse trail to watch it land in the field. Deputy Cranton ran with us. Lightning framed the copter's blades as they scattered brush and dirt. We walked as close as we could to the aircraft. EMTs slid Vicki's stretcher from the ambulance, carried it to the helicopter and eased her inside.

"What will they do at the hospital?" I asked Sam. I wished I could be with Vicki, holding her hand. Someone should be with her. I glanced at River Rat. He stared at the helicopter, evidently not inclined to reveal his identity and ask to go with his sister.

"They'll do blood work," Sam said, "head and body scans, monitor her vital signs, help her breathe, put EKG leads on her chest to monitor her heart."

Stunned, we watched the helicopter rise into the sky amid rumbling thunder. Sporadic lightning flashed near the copter's blades. I held my breath until the helicopter disappeared. The ambulance pulled away.

Deputy Cranton said, "So the girl's horse threw her? Did anybody see what made the horse pitch?"

Everybody shook their heads.

"Who was last to see her before this happened?" Nobody moved or spoke. Lightning crackled across the sky. I hoped Vicki's copter pilot wasn't flying through bolts.

"I'd like to see you all in the dining hall," Cranton said.

A thunder crash propelled us toward the lodge. Droplets of rain began to fall. As we hustled to the building, Meredith and I shot an inquisitive glance at Sam. He touched a finger to his lips.

"Okay," I said.

"Right." Meredith nodded.

Judging from the determined set of his jaw, I thought he'd decided to stay undercover and investigate why Vicki fell. But I had to make sure. While everybody scrambled toward the lodge, I whispered in his ear. "You're going to stay incognito to find out what happened to Vicki?"

He nodded. Determination oozed from him. I shared it. We couldn't possibly leave.

Ranger overtook us and loped past. "That dang horse Vicki rides spooks at noises. 'Specially in stormy weather."

Nineteen

The entire group of us crammed ourselves through the front door of the lodge.

"I need your names and contact information," the deputy said. "Tell me when you last saw Vicki Landsdale and anything else you know about her. Line up here, please."

My feet started itching. "Let's be near the front of the line," I whispered to Meredith. "Then we can go back to the trail and search around."

"Are you crazy? That's the deputy's job. Besides, it's about to storm."

"We need to comb the area before it starts pouring and the rain washes everything away."

"Washes what away? I'm not even going to tell Sam you said that."

I was thankful she wouldn't tell Sam, but Vicki's injuries felt personal. She'd become a friend. I had to help her. Not even her brother would come forward. Even if nobody else cared about her, I did. How could I abandon her? Guilt would overwhelm me. I knew. I'd done it before—abandoned people closer to me than Vicki. I'd never do it again.

It looked as though Sam and I were never going to have ordinary time together without a tragedy occurring in our midst. We could never have a relationship without some emergency forcing us together. The whole idea Sam and I could ever be close was a silly figment of my imagination.

But there was no way we could leave the ranch. Somebody who didn't like Vicki might have caused her fall. If I found something significant where the horse threw her, I'd tell Sam. He had the expertise to evaluate the information. If he grew angry, I'd be satisfied knowing I'd done the right thing. I'd developed my own sense of duty.

Meredith and I were near the front of the line and among the first to be interviewed. It didn't take us long to tell the deputy that Vicki had left dinner early. I didn't tell him Wayne Rickoff and the Tensels left soon after she did, nor did I mention her troubles with other cowboys and her brother. I had to believe she'd recover and could tell the deputy herself. Meredith and I moved aside so he could question the others.

My curiosity bubbled to the surface. I had an idea. I saw a chance to make a discovery before trekking back to the horse trail.

"Meredith, after the sheriff finishes questioning each person, why don't you slip over and charm that person into telling you where they were between dinner and Selma's screams? Bat your eyes. Say you're terribly interested in their experience for an article."

"Are you determined to get us into this? Are you actually going back to that trail?"

"Okay, okay. I shouldn't go back. Here come Ranger and Monty. Just smile and find out where they went after dinner." I turned her around and practically pushed her in front of the two men.

Before she could protest, I scurried toward the door, slipped outside the lodge and headed for the corrals.

Twenty

On a list of people who didn't like Vicki, Ranger (when she ignored his flirting) and Monty would be near the top. While Meredith chatted with those two in the lodge, maybe I could find something at the corrals to tie them to Vicki's fall.

The sky was menacing, but at least rain wasn't pouring yet. I jogged at a pretty good clip but slowed down when I neared the enclosure. The horses milled around, spooky from the weather. Lightning cracked. The horses stiffened and laid back their ears. When thunder rumbled, they blew air out of their nostrils and whirled aimlessly in half circles.

I neared the corral, talking in soothing tones like the wranglers did. My utterances seemed to work. The horses grew still, studied me and puffed. I didn't relish sharing space with the skittish creatures, but I saw a shiny object lying in the dirt in front of the horses.

Talking steadily in reassuring tones, I eased through the corral gate. At first, the horses stood their ground. Then they tossed their heads and backed up. When I bent to retrieve the shiny item, one horse snorted and whipped around, placing his backside toward me. It was Marbach, the horse Monty said kicked at noises behind him. Praying his flying hooves couldn't reach me, I snatched up the item and skedaddled backward toward the gate.

Another horse pranced in my direction, whinnying and showing her teeth. I thought she wanted to take a piece out of my arm. I spun and sprinted for the gate. Just before I squeezed through, her teeth caught my billowing skirt. I shoved the gate closed and whirled around. Fabric from my sundress hung from the horse's lips.

If I hadn't been working out, she'd have chomped my derriere. I reached back and felt a hole in my skirt.

Still panting, I opened my palm to see what I'd retrieved from the corral: a piece of wire about two inches long. Ranger's sculpture wire? I dropped it into my pocket, inhaled a liter of air and began trotting back toward the lodge. The air felt like soup. Droplets fell intermittently.

When I spotted Deputy Cranton ambling toward his patrol car, I slipped behind a tree. I didn't want him wondering what I was doing outside in inclement weather with my poison ivy patch exposed through a ripped skirt.

Once his car pulled out of sight, I scurried to the lodge and stopped to take a breath before I entered. Holding my shoulders back, I surreptitiously pulled my skirt closed behind me as I slipped into the lodge. Everybody in the dining room sat quietly with somber faces.

I walked to the bench were Sam and Meredith sat. Sam looked up at me and raised his eyebrows.

"I needed to get some air and snagged my dress on a bush."

Meredith gave me a disgusted look. She knew I'd been sneaking around somewhere, but she apparently hadn't told Sam. I eased my tailbone onto the bench.

Bertha was giving a pep talk about why everyone should stay and enjoy the ranch despite the accident. Until that moment, I didn't know she was capable of such charm.

"Vicki's going to be all right," she said. "And don't worry about her horse. Nobody but the wranglers will be allowed to ride it. Tonight's rain will make the weather cooler tomorrow. It'll be the most perfect Hill Country day you ever saw." She floated down to her chair, smiling.

Sam whispered under his breath, "She's desperate to keep everybody happy. She has a lot at stake here."

George Tensel stood. "I think we should all go home. What happened here tonight is a bad omen." He'd never looked to me like a man concerned with omens.

Bertha jumped up. "Y'all paid up front for an authentic ranch holiday. I want you to enjoy it." She smiled. "Besides, I don't give refunds."

George sat.

"It's too late to decide anything tonight," Bertha purred. "Why don't we all go to bed, listen to the soothin' rain when it comes, get a good night's sleep and meet here for Maria's scrumptious breakfast in the morning."

We were too tired to protest. Nobody had the energy to pack up and strike out in the dead of night with a storm brewing.

Bertha's plan sounded superb to me. With everyone staying at the ranch, the usual routine would continue, and I'd have more time to casually nose around.

Twenty-One

As we walked to our cabins, the night air seemed lighter. The bright moon peeking through pewter clouds would reflect enough light off the river for me to scrutinize the area where Vicki fell. A short trip to the trail shouldn't be too dangerous. If somebody caused Vicki's fall, surely the perpetrator wouldn't dare return to the scene. The backs of my thighs felt almost normal. When I thought about clues I might find, my feet itched.

This was my best chance to get evidence. Once everybody got in bed, I could slip out of the cabin. They wouldn't even know I was gone.

To prepare for bed, I donned my Garfield nightshirt. I planned to slip back into my ventilated sundress for sleuthing. Wearing pants would irritate the backs of my legs, and I didn't want extraneous stimulation capturing my attention while I scoured the scene.

Over the dress, I'd wear the jacket I packed; it had pockets for whatever I might find. I'd bought quart-sized Ziploc bags and sterile gloves at Walgreen's and packed them in my suitcase to use in the unlikely event I was called upon to collect evidence.

As soon as Meredith slipped under the covers and turned her face to the wall, I tiptoed to my suitcase, changed, slipped gloves and Ziplocs into my coat pockets and sneaked out the front door. It was lighter outside than I'd hoped. There was no thunder. A gentle mist fell. I darted down the path toward the river, ignoring sounds of night critters foraging nearby in the brush.

When I reached the spot on the trail where Vicki fell, a glimmer caught my eye. Another piece of wire? Pausing, I squinted at the object to make sure it wasn't attached to a snake. It was definitely a piece of wire. Pulling on a glove, I squatted to retrieve the specimen and eased it into a bag. This wire was thinner, different from the corral sample.

I spotted a snatch of fur nearby and bagged it separately. Had an animal spooked Vicki's horse?

Hearing movement in the brush, I froze. A horrible musk smell wafted by me. I held my nose. Was that the odor Vicki described when we first walked to the cabins? A pack of javelinas must be padding through brush somewhere to my right. They had a keen sense of smell and nasty dispositions, but since the breeze had blown their smell in my direction, I doubted they could smell me. They were unlikely to attack me unless I provoked them, which I wasn't about to do. As long as I stayed on the open trail, they were even less likely to approach. I hoped the sound of their teeth gnashing meant they were gorging on a prickly pear cactus. Standing still as stone, I finally heard them pad away through the underbrush.

By the time I thought it was safe to breathe, my eyes had adjusted to moonlight. I saw something else lying in the path: a two-inch piece of rope with a tiny snip of wire stuck to it. The deputy either hadn't seen it or considered it unimportant. Wire, rope, and animal hair were so common on ranches, he wouldn't have considered these items unusual.

The lawman assumed Vicki's horse threw her as a natural reflex to unexpected movement or sound...like a pack of javelinas moving through the brush. Why would he look for evidence of a crime?

Farther ahead, near the spot from where the deputy had retrieved a rock, I spotted a smaller rock dotted with red splatters. Had Vicki hit her head on that rock? Had somebody hit her with it?

Just as I slid the bagged rock into my pocket, a flashlight beam danced toward me through the trees. My heart leaped into my throat. I scurried backward into the brush, praying the javelinas were far away and that my poison ivy patch didn't hit a branch.

Sunny came into view. Why was he here? His makeup looked smeared, as though he'd swiped his hand across it. He walked slowly, scouring the horse trail left and right with his gaze. He walked toward the spot where Vicki had lain and stared at the ground.

Beyond Sunny, from farther down the trail, George Tensel appeared. When he realized there was someone ahead of him, he stopped and shined his flashlight beam on Sunny. I backed deeper into the brush, terrified his light might reflect off the white of my sundress and expose me.

"What's going on here?" George said.

Sunny squinted into the light and didn't answer.

Tensel lowered his flashlight. Relieved, I watched him wave it over horseshoe marks slashed in the dust. Had Vicki's horse danced in reaction to booming thunder? Had it spooked when it heard a shot fired? I saw another cluster of horseshoe marks closer to the rocks where I thought Vicki had hit the ground.

"What are you doing here?" George said.

"What are you doing here, Tensel?" Sunny snapped.

"Trying to figure out what happened to the girl." They scowled at each other. George flashed his light in wider arcs over the ground, lifting it again in my direction. I eased farther back into the brush. George lowered the light back to the area where Vicki fell. They stared at the illuminated patch of earth. Neither man spoke.

Finally, George cleared his throat. "I can't tell much here. Selma's still in a frenzy. I need to get back and see if I can calm her down."

Sunny wiped his hand across his face. "I need to check the campfire. Make sure it's out."

"I'm sure the girl will be fine," George said. "People fall off horses all the time."

"Yes," Sunny mumbled. "She should be all right." They turned and walked back the way they'd come.

When they were out of sight, I concentrated on getting my breathing back to normal. Had one of them come back to search for evidence of what he'd done? I fingered my pockets. I didn't know the significance of what I found, but I was glad I found it before they did.

If George or Sunny caused Vicki's fall, I might find something incriminating in their cabins. But George was on the way to his cabin to calm Selma, and Sam occupied the adjoining cabin. Sneaking around that habitat was out of the question.

When their footsteps receded and I could no longer see flashlight beams, I eased out of the brush, listening for sounds of movement. The night was still. Even the animals must be hunkered down, awaiting the storm.

It occurred to me that Sam was apt to show up. I decided I better hightail it back to my cabin before he appeared and started lecturing me about being there. I wanted to evaluate my contraband, not relinquish it.

Sunny said he had chores to complete. I remembered from looking at the map that his cabin wasn't far from ours. Maybe I had time to check out Sunny's cabin before returning to mine.

Twenty-Two

Just as I remembered, Sunny's cabin stood between ours and the main lodge. The small building was nestled in a secluded grove of oak trees. A narrow limestone footpath led to his door. The windows were partially open, but the cabin was dark. I stood still in the brush long enough to ascertain Sunny wasn't there. Then I darted for the door, opened it and tiptoed inside. Once my eyes adjusted, I saw a bureau across the room with a piece of paper folded on top. I scurried over, grabbed the paper and unfolded it. The words I read appeared to have been scrawled in haste: "Just in case. Fulfill your dreams. Vicki #0746."

A map lay beside the paper.

I drew closer and recognized the Caribbean Sea. There was a dot on the sea north of St. Kitts. I squinted. Was it a reef? A tiny island?

Besides me, Sunny had appeared to be Vicki's only friend at the ranch. At least, he'd taken up for her after the snake incident. Had she confided to him she wanted to disappear to a remote island near St. Kitts?

Now that Vicki was injured and might never be able to go, Sunny might be tempted to take advantage of the "just in case" scenario she scribbled on her note. Vicki told me she deposited funds somewhere. Maybe the number in her note led to the funds she stashed.

Did Sunny decide he couldn't wait to fulfill his dreams, whatever they were? With Vicki out of the way, maybe he could chase dreams in the Caribbean without her.

Cans of face paint were lined up in front of the map. I withdrew the bag from my pocket with the spattered rock and held it next to a can of red paint. As best I could tell in semi-darkness, the colors matched. The front door of the cabin slammed back against the frame. My heart catapulted to my throat. Slipping the bag into my pocket, I whirled around.

"What are you doing in here?" Sunny roared.

My heart skipped a beat. I backed up to his bureau.

He glowered. "How dare you come into my cabin!"

"I... I... went for a walk, got turned around in the dark and came upon your cabin. The girls twitter about you all the time... they think you're so handsome. When I realized this was your cabin, I have to admit I got curious."

I froze, awaiting his response. He was between me and the door. How could I get past him? While he considered what to do, I decided to make my move. I strode toward him, shaking my head apologetically.

"I'm sorry. I shouldn't have come in uninvited. I'll just go now and leave you in peace."

It wasn't that easy. Before I could reach the door, he grabbed my shoulders and leaned into my face. His fingers dug into my flesh.

"What do you want in here? What do you want with me? Do you think I scared Vicki's horse? Is that it?" His eyes were fireballs. "How dare you!" He shook me.

I pressed against his chest with all my strength. My pushing was useless. He was bigger and stronger than I realized. Moonlight coming through the door lit the scar on his face like a slash of evil.

He gripped powerful fingers deeper into my shoulders. It hurt. I had to think fast. Quick as lightning, I poked his eye with my finger and scratched his face.

"Ouch!" He let loose.

I scrambled out the door and ran, praying he was too busy dealing with his eye to come after me. I was picking up speed when I crashed into Sam and nearly knocked us both down.

Twenty-Three

"Agatha. What in God's name are you doing out here?"

"I couldn't sleep after all the excitement," I panted. "I was out walking, but it didn't help." I had to suck air between words. "I thought jogging...might make me... tired enough to sleep."

His eyes narrowed. "If someone spooked Vicki's horse, they could still be out here." He deliberately pronounced each word making my heart freeze. "Are you out of your mind?"

I hated it when he said that. He should know better. He he thought he knew everything and nobody else could figure anything out. He'd be impressed with what I found. If I decided to tell him.

I hadn't forgotten what happened at the health club. Things got dicey when I exposed the killer. Yet, Sam never once expressed appreciation for my help.

Right now, I didn't want him checking my pockets. I needed to deflect his questions. Making an instantaneous decision, I clasped my hands behind his neck.

"I'm frightened," I said, clinging there. Our faces nearly touched. I kissed him hard.

He was astonished. He was also a little damp from the mist. I loved the smell of his Old Spice Aftershave mixed with rain. I felt him relax. I think he forgot to be angry. He reached around my back and pulled me closer.

I hoped he didn't lower his arm farther down than my jacket and discover the hole in my dress.

I knew kissing him to distract him was a crummy thing to do. But it was wonderful. The two of us. Alone. Under the night sky. I relaxed into him.

His whole body stiffened, and he backed away. "If there's any investigating to be done, I'll do it. You can't get involved."

I was afraid he might feel that way. Before he could crank up more indignation, I snuggled in closer and touched my mouth tentatively to his. He responded and held me even tighter.

My previous resolve to stall our relationship and concentrate on doing the right thing flew into the atmosphere. I could hardly breathe.

Unfortunately, I could still think. When I sensed his urgency, I felt totally ashamed for leading him on.

Then the backs of my legs started itching.

I thought about the goodies in my pockets.

It took all my strength to push Sam away. When I took a step back, we were both breathless.

"I'm scared to be out here," I panted. "Like you said, somebody might be around."

When he reached for me again, I straightened my arms. "No. You're absolutely right. I shouldn't be here."

He blinked.

I knew I was acting like a first class creep, but I didn't know what else to do. I didn't have the courage to be honest.

"We need to go to our cabins." I spun around, holding my skirt closed in back, and took off.

"Hey, wait. What the...?"

No way was I going to wait. Even though I'd moved up to forty-five minutes on the treadmill, by the time I reached my cabin, I was heaving like a basketball forward.

I slithered inside, quietly locked the door and went straight to my suitcase. I retrieved the "Do Not Disturb" sign I'd snitched from a hotel and carried with me in case of emergency. There were times when a person did not want to be disturbed and did not want to answer questions.

Tiptoeing back to the door, I eased it open and peeked through the crack. When I didn't see anybody, I slipped the sign on the door handle and maneuvered the door closed. Leaning against the door, I closed my eyes and asked God's forgiveness for acting like an idiot. I tried to formulate specific promises about honesty and about my future behavior, but my heart wasn't in it.

Careful not to wake Meredith, I lifted a chair and wedged it under the knob without making a sound.

Scraping Sunny's face paint from under my nails, I flicked the spatters into a fourth Ziploc bag and dropped it with other bags into the empty suitcase under my bed.

When I went to the bathroom to wash and treat my poison ivy patch, I noticed that my face was still swollen. Maybe Sam would conclude I'd suffered an allergic reaction that caused temporary insanity. Hopefully, my kisses would not make his face swell.

I heard two of the girls snoring and Jangles talking in her sleep. I tried to make out what Jangles said. I'd have enjoyed hearing her babble about what she and Ranger were doing earlier in the evening. Unfortunately, I couldn't decipher her giggly gibberish.

I finally crept to bed, easing sideways onto my bunk to let my itchy patch dry. When I thought about Sam, my lips tingled. He might be so angry he'd never speak to me again.

I made myself consider who would want to hurt Vicki. Why did Sunny return to the spot where she fell? Did his wearing makeup relate in any way to Vicki? Was he really an empathetic person? He sure didn't seem like one when he was digging his fingers into my shoulders.

What was he hiding besides that scar? When Vicki signed the note I found in his cabin, what did she mean by "just in case?" Had she feared an attack?

What did the numbers on her note signify? Had Sunny promised to go with her to that dot in the Caribbean? Had he decided to do her in so he could abscond to the island by himself and get his hands on her "untraceable" money?

Maybe George Tensel had chased after Vicki and tried to get her to dismount. When Vicki refused, George jerked the horse's reins and Vicki tugged back. Her horse, spooked from the jerking and yelling, threw her. George might have returned to the trail to look for evidence that implicated him but was thwarted by Sunny's arrival.

Selma left dinner right after George did. What if she finally caught him trying to make time with Vicki, and she spooked the horse?

I could still feel the warmth of Sam's arms tightening around my back. My skin prickled. I was finding it increasingly hard to think. How could I investigate without irritating him? I just wanted him to trust me. I thought he wanted to trust me. Admittedly, my spontaneous actions made it difficult.

I tried to concentrate on more suspects. Bertha hated Vicki's youth and beauty and seethed with jealousy over the attention Ranger paid her, but she depended on the girl. Vicki's accident made it hard for Bertha to keep everybody at the ranch.

I wondered, incidentally, if Bertha knew how much Ranger enjoyed having Jangles chase after him.

Had I found Ranger's sculpting wire? According to Monty, Ranger had designs on this ranch, and Monty stood to benefit. Had they concluded they'd both be better off with Vicki out of the picture?

If Wayne Rickoff fired his gun to spook Vicki's horse, nobody could have distinguished a shot from all that thunder. Not even Jangles.

My mind flipped back to Sam. Having managed to keep the clues I gathered away from him, I would dazzle him at the right moment with my crime-solving prowess. Assuming he still spoke to me.

I would become invaluable to his investigation. Meanwhile, I had to keep from infuriating him. My grabbing him, then running away, undoubtedly ticked him off. Sometimes a person like me gets desperate.

That thought led me to River Rat. Did his addictions make him desperate? How far would he go to get his sister's money?

My evaluation of suspects wasn't productive. I couldn't keep my mind off Sam. If only I could get him to trust me. I didn't seem to be making any headway creating trust.

Sunny Barlow and I both used facades. In the long run, I had to admit that our facades probably wouldn't work.

Blessed rains finally came. As I listened to splatters hit the roof, I hugged myself. I imagined Sam's arms wrapped around me and prayed to high heaven I hadn't alienated him forever.

Twenty-Four

At the first hint of dawn, I peeked through the door and brought in the hotel "Do Not Disturb" sign. I toted the chair back to the table and sneaked back to my bunk. Not long after daylight, everyone started moving around, but nobody talked. Even our suitemates were silent. We were all worried about Vicki and wondering whether Bertha and George would have another shouting match at breakfast about whether everyone should stay at the ranch. Our vacation looked doomed.

I stitched up the hole in the back of my dress and put it back on. I was getting pretty sick of the billowy thing.

We were all sitting outside at the table under the oak when Sam and the Tensels walked up. Sam's expression was resolute. I hoped he hadn't changed his mind about investigating incognito. He might have decided to let Bandera County authorities determine why and how Vicki fell. If the deputy sheriff assumed Vicki suffered an accident, a conclusion he might easily reach, we might never learn the truth.

We plodded to the dining hall like mourners headed for a grave site. I don't remember if birds were singing. Sam wouldn't even look at me.

In the dining hall, everyone stood around, quiet with anticipation. As soon as everybody'd gone through the breakfast line and found a table, Bertha stood and cleared her throat.

"I know we're all concerned about Vicki." A hush fell. "She's at San Antonio University Hospital, still unconscious. She can't have visitors." Despondent sighs rippled through the room. "But doctors expect her to recover." We sat straighter. People inhaled.

"Her parents are flying to San Antonio. Let's pray for the best." She smiled and settled herself on her bench.

I glanced at Sam. His face was inscrutable.

Utensils clicked, interspersed with the murmur of subdued chatter. Nobody talked to me, so I decided I might as well focus on food. When we finished eating, I asked Meredith for the pad and pencil she always carried and walked over to Bertha.

"I'd like to send a card to Vicki and her parents at the hospital. Can you tell me their names?"

"Steve and Marcia Landsdale."

As I returned to the table, Sam pushed back his chair. "I feel like taking a walk."

Since he'd finally spoken, I decided I better respond.

"Me, too." Uninvited, I jumped up and followed him. When he pushed open the lodge door, I barely swished through before it slammed shut.

Sam strode briskly down the main road toward the ranch entrance. It was all I could do to keep up.

He must be furious with me for having teased him. He'd suffered the pain of losing his family. Now he had to deal with a meddling, obstreperous twit—me—complicating the rest of his life. He was never going to speak to me again. He was walking out of my life.

He whirled and glared at me.

"I don't buy it," he said.

I froze and sucked in a breath. "Buy what?"

"What Bertha said about Vicki."

"Why not?" I tried to figure out what he was talking about, gauge his expression, and keep from crying while my heart tried to explode.

"She was just thrown from the horse last night. They're still doing tests this morning. How could Bertha know the doctors expect her to recover?"

My mouth started moving. "She's almost like a relative. Maybe Bertha contacted her doctors early this morning."

"It's too soon. Vicki was unconscious. Doctors wouldn't know the extent of her injuries yet."

"I see what you mean."

He started walking. We reached the front gate, he opened it, and we walked through. We'd gone a few yards farther down the road when he whirled to face me again. My heart stopped.

"Hand it over," he said.

"Hand what over?"

"Whatever you found that you didn't want to discuss when you started kissing me last night."

My stomach churned like an eggbeater. "How do you know I found anything?"

"You were snooping around at the place where Vicki fell. Hand it over."

He sounded firm but not hateful. My heartbeat slowed. I wanted to keep the clues to myself until I was sure I'd found something significant. But I didn't know how I was going to accomplish that feat. I stalled.

"If I found anything, which I didn't, I certainly wouldn't keep it with me."

"Yes, you would," he said. "You'd be afraid to leave evidence in your room."

I hated the way he read my mind. I reached in my pockets, retrieved the contraband and handed it over: wire, rope, fur, rock, and flecks of clown paint from underneath my nails, each in a plastic bag.

"Good. You kept the items separate." I exhaled.

"You have her parents' names?" I handed him the paper.

"I'll call my SAPD buddy." He put each sample carefully in his pockets, then patted the pistol holstered on his hip under the loose shirt. "Let's walk farther away from the ranch."

He took off with long strides, pulled his cell phone from another pocket and dialed. "Hey, pal. Can you talk?"

I practically jogged to keep up.

The guy on the other end of the wire apparently knew Sam's voice. I heard him respond. "Yeah. What's going on?"

Sam lowered his voice. "I'm relaxing on vacation in the Hill Country and didn't reveal I'm a cop. I think a crime might have been committed here last night. I want to interview the parents of an injured girl. They're flying from Wisconsin to San Antonio today: Steve and Marcia Landsdale. Can you get me their airline and flight number? Time of arrival?"

"No problem. I'll leave the info on your cell. You need backup?"

"No. I'm good. I need to keep this confidential. But I may come to town this afternoon to use my computer."

"I'll be out of the station. I'll tell the dispatcher that you're still on vacation but might come in."

He clicked off and turned to me. "That was good work, you getting the names of Vicki's parents. Makes it easy to find them and interview them."

I beamed. In addition to appreciating my efforts, he'd forgotten to be angry.

I was on a roll.

"What about the evidence samples? Can your friend send them to forensics?" I asked.

"No, he'd have to file a CIL form to ask the crime lab to conduct tests and put a case number on the samples. We don't want to go that route. We don't even know for sure that we're looking at a crime here."

If we didn't have a crime, why did my feet itch more than my poison ivy patch?

"My friend at the crime lab might be able to help," he said. He dialed another number, described the evidence in low tones and clicked off.

"He said to bring in what we found. He'll take a look."

"You have to take me with you to San Antonio," I said.

"Why should I do that?"

"They're my samples. I found them. Plus, I talked to Vicki a lot. We hit it off. Her parents are more apt to trust me."

"Another cross for those poor people to bear."

I ignored his remark. "If Meredith and I hadn't invited you here, you wouldn't even know about this case. I talked you into coming, remember?"

"How could I forget?" He whipped around and headed back toward the ranch, marching several feet ahead of me with a determined stride. "You have an intriguing sense of logic, Agatha."

He hadn't called me Agatha since I crashed into him on the horse trail. Before that, he called me Agatha when I confronted murder suspects at the health club after he warned me not to get involved. His calling me Agatha was not a good sign.

We walked all the way back to the ranch entrance, went through the gate and could see the outline of the lodge roof in the distance before he spoke. When he turned to face me, his jaw was set.

I must have blown it. He looked so stern, I had to clench my fists to keep from sticking fingers in my ears. I didn't want to hear what he was about to say. "Let Meredith know what's happening," he said. "Tell her we'll be back late this afternoon."

He was going to take me with him! Before he could change his mind, I ran back to our cabin and motioned Meredith to step outside so the girls wouldn't overhear.

"Vicki's fall might not have been accidental," I said. "I'm going with Sam to San Antonio to meet her parents—see if we can learn anything. I'll take my laptop if you don't need it."

"Sure."

"If anybody misses us, tell them we went to Bandera for toiletries and will be back late today."

"I'm going horseback riding this morning. Maybe I can get information out of the wranglers— learn whether Vicki's horse had any quirks besides being afraid of loud noises."

It was great having a snooping partner. Meredith's precision with details was stupendous.

"Be careful, okay? Who else is going on the ride?"

"Selma's going. She didn't want to get back in the river."

As soon as the girls left for their morning swim with River Rat, I packed my laptop, treated my poison ivy and put on my baggiest jeans and shirt. I stuffed my pockets with necessities and strolled to Sam's car. I paused nonchalantly to look around, then jumped in and slumped down in case anybody walked by. I didn't want to arouse suspicions about why we would leave and return the same day, so close to the end of our vacation.

Where was Sam?

Twenty-Five

Just when I was sure he'd changed his mind, Sam swung into the seat. He'd barely eased the car through the entrance gate when he started grousing. "I still can't believe you went back to where Vicki fell, alone, in the dark."

Since his face was getting red, I kept quiet. "Those pieces of evidence you found: did it occur to you if somebody spooked Vicki's horse, whoever it was might go back and look for exactly what you found?"

I kept my face impassive with a mere hint of harmony to acknowledge he might be on to something.

"If somebody tried to kill Vicki and you showed up, they wouldn't have hesitated to kill you, too." Those words scared me. I had to swallow before I could speak.

"Actually, George and Sunny did show up." I described how I hid while they looked over the area and left.

"If one of them was the killer...and he showed up alone...and he found you..." Sam pulled on to the shoulder and stopped the car. He reached across the seat and grabbed my shoulders.

"Look, Aggie, we both meant those kisses last night—even if you were trying to distract me." He looked straight at me. "I know that's what you were doing."

I felt my face flush and looked down.

"I care about you, Aggie. You know that. I understand you have this compulsion to learn about everything, but you can't leap into dangerous situations without thinking. You'll get hurt."

The “without thinking” part irritated me. He drew me into his arms. I smiled and closed my eyes.

He held me tighter. “I didn’t think I could care about anyone else after losing Katy and Lee. Then you came along.” He seemed torn about that. He loosened his embrace.

“You loved them, too,” he said. Then his voice cracked. His grief had returned. He released me and sank back against the seat.

I felt my armor cracking and swallowed to regain control. “I did love them.”

Being around Sam again, I realized I’d loved him from way back when he and Katy were married. But moving to Texas after Sam did might have been a bad idea. Losing Katy and Lee had broken both our hearts. I wasn’t sure two broken hearts could mend well enough to love again.

He looked so miserable, I couldn’t help myself. I slid closer to him, reached over and patted his chest. He looked surprised and then suspicious. He put his arm around me, but our moment had passed.

I twisted around to look into his eyes. “I’ll be careful, Sam. I was stupid to go out there alone. It’s just that I get so eager. I feel this urgency to know what happened, especially to someone I care about.”

“I know.” He nodded, exhaled and seemed relieved.

I relaxed into the curve of his arm. I’d loved him for so long. At eighteen, I’d thought I loved Lester. What did I know about love back then?

The mere thought of falling in love again must terrify Sam. He worshipped Katy and Lee and lost them. He might fear that daring to love again would diminish their memory.

What if something happened to yet another person he loved? How could he risk the pain of enduring more loss?

That’s when it hit me.

The reason he got so irritated when I thrust myself into investigations wasn’t merely because he thought I should keep quiet and stay out of his way. It was because he’d loved deeply before and couldn't prevent Katy and Lee's deaths. He was terrified it might happen again.

There was still the secret from our lives back in Chicago that he must never know. If he found out, our chances of ever being together would be destroyed.

I knew I'd eventually reveal to him what I'd done. Somehow, I'd find the courage to risk rejection. Someday, I'd find and deliver words that would either bind us together or rip us irrevocably apart.

We couldn't go on indefinitely as we were. We'd crossed a threshold. I didn't possess enough backbone to risk disclosure, but I prayed courage would come. I had to believe that, at some point, our relationship would be strong enough for me to think he could love me in spite of the past.

Meanwhile, for us to have any kind of relationship, I had to be helpful without making him fear for my safety. If he was able to love again, I'd be there. I was making progress.

"Now that we're working together," I said, "if I find anything else, I'll bring it to you. I promise." I did not intend to lie. Why did my feet itch?

He tightened his arm around my shoulder, like a pal. "I wish we weren't always working to solve a crime," he said. "We could enjoy some normal time together...if you didn't have that aversion to normalcy." He looked down at me and grinned.

I smiled back. "You'd be bored."

"Maybe," he said.

He cranked the engine and veered the Caprice back onto the highway.

Twenty-Six

Sam steered the car higher through hills before the highway began a gradual descent back toward San Antonio. He and I weren't having the quiet vacation I'd hoped for, but at least we were together. He was including me.

Our methods might be different, but we shared a compulsion to find justice for victims.

I relayed all I knew about Max and Billy Sue Vernons' deaths near the drilling site. "Even though Herb was their son," I said, "they left the ranch to their niece Bertha because she loved it so."

"I don't imagine that sat well with Herb."

"No, it didn't. He's still furious with Bertha. When Bertha treated my poison ivy, I heard him arguing with her about the ranch."

"The Vernons were not elderly and died unexpectedly? Authorities would have autopsied their bodies," he said.

"Vicki said Bertha didn't like to talk about it. She did say Billy Sue exercised constantly to stay thin and that walking back to the lodge shouldn't have been difficult for her. According to Maria, they'd ridden around and hiked all day a couple of days earlier without incident. Maria made them sandwiches and Max wanted extra thermoses of water. The day after they spent roaming the ranch, they went to San Antonio on business and returned home late that afternoon. Their son Herb arrived at the ranch that same day, stayed overnight and left early the next morning. On the day they died."

"Did Vicki know if authorities did toxicology tests on the Vernons or their thermoses?" he asked.

"We didn't talk about that. But when I met Herb Vernon and his wife Bitsy at the lodge, I gathered Herb thought the ranch should be his. I heard him badger Bertha to let energy companies drill on the property. He owns half the mineral rights. Bertha owns the other half and the executive rights, so she'd be the one to lease the land to an oil company. She's against drilling. Wants to keep the ranch as it is."

"Interesting. Especially since Bertha has to work so hard maintaining the place as a dude ranch."

I didn't tell him how menacing Herb was when he accosted me outside the lodge. Now that Sam and I were working together, I didn't want to give him another reason why we should leave.

"I found the Vernons' obituary online," I said. "Herb and Bertha are their only living relatives. Herb apparently never liked living on the ranch. Once his parents sent him to school in San Antonio, he never came back much over the years. Maria told me that. Which makes it even stranger that he happened to come back the night before his parents died."

He rubbed his chin. "I'll see what I can learn about the Vernons' deaths at SAPD. Bandera doesn't have a medical examiner, so the couple would have been sent to San Antonio for autopsy. Maybe I can see a copy of those reports. By the way, did you bring that map of the ranch?"

"Sure did."

He stuck it in his pocket. His cell phone rang. "Yeah. Thanks, buddy, for the flight information." Sam clicked a button to save the call.

We drove straight to the airport and parked as close we could to the flight arrival terminal. At the baggage claim, we didn't have long to wait. An attractive couple with pinched faces stood waiting for luggage. The woman had Vicki's pretty features. She wore creamy, wrinkle-free linen that highlighted her smooth complexion, which had probably been enhanced with Retin-A and cosmetic peels. I hoped grief wasn't about to diminish her beauty.

A red silk power tie set off her husband's lightweight wool-and-silk navy sport coat. He paced around luggage conveyer belts rubbing his hand across his chin like a man impatient with unpleasant surprises and interrupted schedules. This couple had to be Steve and Marcia Landsdale.

Sam walked up and introduced himself as a San Antonio detective vacationing incognito at the ranch where Vicki worked. He introduced me as Vicki's friend and a guest at the ranch. We expressed our condolences about Vicki's accident. Sam said we questioned whether her fall was accidental and asked them to protect his cover so he could investigate.

"Why would anyone want to hurt Vicki?" Steve asked.

"We don't know that they did. We're just checking possibilities."

"Vicki has begun to enjoy herself at the ranch, hasn't she?" Marcia asked.

"Yes, I think she has," I said. It was only a partial lie. "She does a good job and works hard to keep the guests happy. She's grown to care about the place. She loves riding the horses."

Why should I tell them I knew about River Rat or about Vicki's other conflicts? They clearly loved their daughter, even if they found unusual ways to protect her. There was no point adding to their concern.

"Shouldn't we be at the hospital?" Steve looked at his watch.

"Yes," Sam said. "We need just a few minutes to learn more about Vicki. She was going to college in Wisconsin?"

"When she was younger," Marcia said, "we took Vicki and her brother Trey to the horse fair in Madison. Trey never cared much about horses or college, but Vicki loved horses. She wanted to attend Wisconsin University in Wausheka. The town has a lot of horse farms and rodeos. It's about nineteen miles west of Milwaukee on Highway 94. It's only a little farther from our

Bayview house on Lake Michigan, so we'd have her close by. She was taking general education requirements when she met a boy studying sociology."

"That hippie," Steve fumed. "I never saw him wear anything but faded jeans, T-shirts with holes and flip-flops. Naturally, he had long hair and a beard. Nobody's going to offer a good paying job to a guy who looks like that, unless he's some kind of genius. This guy was no genius."

"Vicki told me that when his sociology class took veterans to rodeos in Milwaukee, her boyfriend took her along," I said.

"That's right," Marcia said. "It was a kind thing for the school to do, but that hippie's classes had nothing to do with Vicki."

"Can't make a living studying sociology," Steve said. "The hippie called himself an artist, but so far as I knew, he never sold anything. We thought if Vicki did some real work for a while, she might appreciate the value of a good education. We'd heard about Texas dude ranches and found out about the BVSBar. The ranch in Bandera, Texas, was as far away from Wisconsin as we could send her without shipping her overseas."

"I see," I said. I remembered my conversation with Vicki the first day she and I walked to the cabins. "If it's any comfort," I told them, "I don't think she cares much about her Wisconsin boyfriend anymore."

"Thank goodness." Marcia sighed. "She doesn't communicate much. We didn't know how she was doing. We sent her brother Trey down to keep an eye on her. Nobody at the ranch knows he's her brother."

"All Trey knows how to do is swim and flirt," Steve said. "We thought he'd fit right in."

Could the Landsdales be oblivious to Trey's fondness for alcohol and drugs? What about his attempt to prey on Vicki?

Marcia's cell phone rang. She turned her back and scrambled through her purse.

"About the veterans her boyfriend's class took to the rodeo," Sam said, "do you know which VA hospital they were from?"

"It wasn't something that interested us."

Marcia, her ear still to the phone, put her hand over her mouth and burst into tears.

"Vicki lapsed into a coma," she cried. "They said to hurry."

Her husband caught her before she collapsed and struggled to carry her to a chair. He blinked back tears.

"Do whatever you need to do, detective," he commanded. "Find the bastard who did this to Vicki."

Twenty-Seven

Sam and I helped the distraught couple hail a cab to San Antonio University Hospital. We drove to SAPD Central on Nueva, stunned into silence from learning Vicki was in a coma.

Since it was almost noon, we maneuvered through Jack in the Box's drive-through on the way and got two bacon ultimate cheeseburgers with Cokes. Sam had scarfed down his burger before we arrived at SAPD's parking lot.

The air was fairly cool from the recent rain. I told Sam if he'd park in the shade, I'd finish my burger, fire up my laptop, and see what I could learn about Vicki's college taking veterans to rodeos. I might also glean tidbits about wire used on ranches and horse behavior.

"I need to know about clowning and clown makeup," I said, "and about drilling for oil and gas in Texas," I said. "I'll enjoy surfing the net again." Even though Meredith and I had only been out of classes since mid-May, I missed studying.

"Why research drilling for oil and gas?" he said.

"When I overheard Herb Vernon arguing with Bertha, Herb said he remembered that when he was growing up, an oil well was drilled somewhere on the ranch. He asked Bertha if she'd ever gone to check the site. He thought there might be oil all over the place. She told him if he wanted to go looking for a dry hole, go ahead. She wasn't interested in having anybody drill holes in her land, never had been and never would be. But earlier, when Bertha was treating my poison ivy, I saw a piece of paper in her room that said something about a well."

My other reason for staying in the car was that I felt my face swelling. I'd definitely spread plant poison from my fingers to my face. When I crashed into Sam in the wilderness and planted those kisses on him, I might have transferred a tad of urushiol sap to his lips. I scrutinized his mouth and jaw line. One jowl looked puffy.

He looked at me quizzically, but shrugged, turned and headed for the station. I looked in the vanity mirror. My cheeks looked balloonish. Puffiness around my eyes pulled them sideways. I resembled Wo Fat.

Forty-eight hours had passed since I'd sat in the ivy, so the time for dangerous swelling was past. I wasn't worried about my throat closing so I couldn't breathe. A swollen face and itching feet apparently weren't fatal.

I had more curiosity than four search engines and powered up my laptop. I learned clowns used two types of paint: grease paint and common face paint. Amateur clowns generally used face paint, made of similar ingredients to those in women's makeup. It was easier to apply and remove.

Although it was trickier to apply, professionals used grease paint, available in pots and tubes, because it stayed on longer. Some clowns painted their faces with white or skin-colored paint before painting new features over the base paint. As a professional, Sunny probably used grease paint. Skin-toned grease paint would more effectively cover the scar running down his jaw line.

Next, I researched Vicki's college, Wisconsin University in Wausheka. Their sociology department frequently took patients from the local veteran's hospital to rodeos and other events.

As for who or what had spooked Vicki's horse, I already knew horses spooked at sudden unexpected noises, smells, and movements. They could hear lower and higher frequencies than humans could, and had a superior sense of smell. With eyes set on the sides of its head, a horse had nearly a 350-degree range of vision. With about sixty-five percent of this range being binocular vision, the horse could quickly spot approaching predators. Any number of stimuli could have caused Vicki's horse to pitch her off.

I found general information about drilling for oil and gas in Texas. When about forty-three percent of US savings and loan associations failed in the 1980s and 1990s, banks grew squeamish about making loans. Energy companies found it nearly impossible to obtain financing for drilling operations. Many Texas companies abandoned drilling projects and sold non-producing wells to smaller companies that later made other efforts to drill. If those wells came up dry, smaller companies couldn't afford to plug them. By the early 1990s, thousands of non-producing unplugged wells dotted Texas.

Was that the type of well that lured Max and Billy Sue out on the ranch the day they died?

Since information I found wasn't shedding much light on our investigation, I decided to research anti-aging remedies for my Dear Aggie readers. It was cool in the car, and Sam was still inside the police station.

I typed telomeres into WebCrawler to see what I could find about cap-like ends on our DNA strands. Scientists had linked longer telomeres to extended life spans. If they were right, I could have more time with Sam.

Before I could Ask Jeeves about telomeres, Sam came walking toward the car. I saved my sites and shut down the laptop.

When he slid into the car, I studied his face. He looked like a squirrel who'd stored a pecan in each jowl. Hopefully, that was the extent of his facial swelling caused by my kisses. Otherwise, he might be inclined to find me reprehensible. He started the engine.

"I'm afraid I didn't find much online to help us learn the details of Vicki's attack," I said.

"It's good that you tried," he said. "I called Joaquin at the crime lab to see if he could obtain the Vernons' autopsy reports without written authorization. He said pathologists are usually reluctant to release autopsy findings because of possible future litigation, but he knows one of the docs there pretty well. Since the deaths occurred five years ago, he thought the doc might let him see the reports. He'll try to have them for us when we arrive."

Twenty-Eight

We drove west on IH 10 toward the medical center. A string of buildings lined both sides of the highway. Freeway traffic was bumper-to-bumper. I began to miss open space at the ranch.

The Bexar County Medical Examiner shared a building with the morgue and crime lab on Louis Pasteur. We walked in with our plastic bags concealed in Sam's pockets.

The building smelled of disinfectant.

I put my hand on Sam's arm. "I hope you get to review the Vernons' autopsies," I said, "but I'm not sure I want to hear the details."

"I understand. I'll summarize what's pertinent. Joaquin said he's ready to look at the evidence you found."

Sam asked to see Forensic Scientist Joaquin Salazar. We were directed to Salazar's lab, and Sam introduced him to me. Joaquin courteously pretended I looked normal and led us to a lab table. He didn't seem to notice that Sam's face looked puffy.

Sam laid the bags on the table. "Aggie found these on the trail where the girl's horse threw her."

Joaquin picked up two bags that contained pieces of wire. "These look like 26- and 30-gauge wires—pretty common on a ranch. Can't tell much, though. You can connect a suspect to these wires?"

"One possible suspect uses the thinner wire to make sculptures. But we don't know if he handled the piece we have here," Sam said.

"We'd need DNA samples from this wire and from wire you know the suspect handled. You'd have to send both pieces to forensics to check for a match. It would take a while."

Sam nodded.

Wearing a sterile glove, Joaquin retrieved the piece of rope from the bag. "The rope is a common variety," he said. He saw a snip of thicker wire stuck to it. "The rope and wire could have multiple uses. To connect a suspect to this sample, you'd have to have a piece of matching rope. The suspect's prints or DNA would have to be on both samples."

Joaquin's evaluation didn't surprise Sam. Sam knew he couldn't send the wire or rope to forensics. Not yet. The items I'd found were, by themselves, insignificant.

Sam handed Joaquin the bag containing the red-splattered rock. Joaquin removed the rock and placed it under the microscope. "Some of the marks are paint. Some are blood." He looked up.

"I think Vicki hit her head there," I said. "Can you tell what kind of paint that is?"

"No. I'd have to compare it to other samples."

"Could any of it be face paint?" Sam asked.

"Could be."

"Could it be grease paint like clowns use?" I asked.

"Could be."

I handed him the plastic bag with flecks of paint I'd scratched from Sunny's face. "Do these flecks match the paint on that rock?"

He moved them under the microscope and compared my paint scrapings with the red splatters.

"They match."

Sam and I looked at each other.

He handed Joaquin another bag. "What can you tell us about this snatch of hair?"

Joaquin slid it under the scope. "It's animal hair. It's consistent with hair from a cat...probably pulled out of the animal. There's a small piece of wire on it, too."

I thought about the bobcats hanging from the dining room ceiling. Wire, looped around their necks and under their hind legs, tied the cats to the ceiling. "The hair you're looking at that's consistent with cat hair, was the cat alive?" I asked.

"I don't think so. If this hair was yanked from a live animal, there would be traces of blood on the scalp end."

We thanked him. As I gathered up our samples, Joaquin pulled Sam aside and showed him a file. "These are the autopsy reports."

Sam found an empty table at the other side of the room, grabbed a stool and bent over the stack of papers.

Joaquin and I made small talk about his job while I watched Sam from the corner of my eye and ignored my itching feet. He took forever perusing the documents and scribbling notes on his pad. He finally came over and handed the papers back to Joaquin. "I appreciate your getting these for me. It's good information. Before we leave, would you check to see if anybody at the ME's office received notification of the death of Vicki or Victoria Landsdale?"

Joaquin dialed and asked about the girl. He listened, then hung up. "No death notice has been received. She must still be at a hospital."

I sighed with relief. "Can you call the hospital," I asked Sam, "and find out how she is?"

"They won't tell me her condition. Only whether or not she can talk. The health privacy act Congress enacted last year, HIPAA, prevents the hospital from releasing information. But I'll call the hospital from the car and see what we can find out."

We thanked Joaquin, returned to the parking lot and sat in the car while Sam dialed University Hospital. I leaned my head against the seat while he asked the charge nurse on Vicki's floor about her, thanked the nurse and clicked the phone closed. When he turned toward me, I opened my eyes.

"They say she can't talk. She must still be in a coma." When my eyes grew moist, Sam reached over and grabbed my hand. "When she lay on the ground," he said, "I thought I saw a trickle of blood seeping from her ear. That usually indicates a swelling brain...not a good sign."

I swallowed the tears in my throat. "I need antihistamine to stop my face from swelling anymore," I sniffed, "and Kleenex...low fat yogurt...and a fashion magazine that doesn't show boots and jeans." I'd spotted a drugstore across the street. "I need to walk. Will you pick me up over there?"

I walked to the store, made my purchases while blowing my nose, and got back in Sam's car. He studied my face but didn't say anything.

As we drove back toward IH 10, I spotted a sporting goods store and asked him to stop. "We have that long trail ride coming up. I better get some riding gloves."

He waited outside while I shopped.

Feeling better, I trotted back to the car and threw my package on the back seat. I'd bought long Neoprene gloves that covered my arms. I didn't want to worry about getting scratched up on the ride. The gloves wouldn't be much hotter than wearing a long-sleeved shirt.

He entered the freeway and drove west, climbing back into the Hill Country. "What did you learn from your research?" he asked.

"Nothing new." I looked out the window, feeling useless. As houses grew scarce on the hills, I noticed the cenizo plants had sprouted flowers from the recent rain. "I read that students from Wisconsin College took veterans from Milwaukee's Clement Zablocki VA Medical Center to the rodeo. Zablocki went to high school and college in Milwaukee and was a US Representative from 1949 until he died in 1983. So they named the hospital after him."

Sam looked over dully. "Is there a reason we need to know that?"

I shrugged. "That's what I learned." I hated not having discovered significant information.

I saw a dead animal roadside...couldn't even tell what it had been. "Tell me about the Vernons' autopsies."

"They died from dehydration and heat stroke, like you said. There were no abnormal substances in their systems and no evidence of trauma, except for a few bruises from where they fell."

"How could that be? How could they both just die like that?" We kept hitting dead ends.

"That's what I wondered. Their family physician's name was on the report, so I called him while you were shopping. He told me Max was diabetic. That's why he drank so much water. Billy Sue exercised a lot, so they were probably both dehydrated when they started out. It's not uncommon for healthy people to die of dehydration, especially in a hot climate during summer."

"Did examiners check their lunches and thermoses? Maybe somebody added diuretics." I remembered seeing diuretics, two different kinds, among pill bottles in Bertha's medicine cabinet.

"They checked stomach contents, food remnants and thermoses. Didn't find anything unusual. The doctor said they routinely took diuretics, her for weight control, him for diabetes."

I told Sam that Maria confirmed Herb had been at the ranch the night before they died. "He had plenty of time to dilute diuretics in their thermoses before he left the next morning," I said. "The question is, why would he do that? Maybe the Vernons told him something that night, something that made him decide to kill them."

"Perhaps they told Bertha they intended to leave the ranch to her, and Herb overheard."

"Examiners didn't find an unusually high level of diuretics in the Vernon's bodies or thermoses?" I had to verify this critical point.

"No, but the Vernons' usual doses would make death from dehydration even more likely."

"Did police question everybody who was at the ranch in the days before the Vernons died?" I asked.

"Yes, but when the autopsies showed death from dehydration and heat stroke, they had no reason to hold anybody as murder suspects."

I thought about the Vernons' activities near the time of their deaths. "Maria told me that the day before they headed out to drive over the ranch, the Vernons drove to San Antonio on business."

"Their family doctor gave me their attorney's name," he said. "Maybe he can tell us what was on their minds."

"Maybe they wanted him to change their wills," I said. "Either that, or something they found at the well site precipitated their deaths, something the authorities overlooked." I just wasn't convinced their deaths were accidental.

"At SAPD," Sam said, "I asked how I could get information about that well. One of the guys called a friend at the Railroad Commission in Austin who searched for records of wells drilled on the ranch. He couldn't find records of wells drilled anywhere in that area. He said oil and gas fields weren't typically found in the Hill Country. The closest fields had been in Medina County, south of Bandera County. He printed out a list of those fields for me." He handed me the paper.

I skimmed it and read aloud: "Taylor-Ina field, near Hondo; Devine, Biry, and Irwin; Adams-Olmos field and Bear Creek field, near Devine; Chacon Lake field, four miles south of Natalia. These towns are all south of the BVSBar?" I asked.

"Yes."

"So there was no oil well drilled on BVSBar property? Why did the Vernons say there was? Why did they go there?"

"I don't know," he said.

"We need to find the place where they died."

The medical examiner's report showed the

location, latitude and longitude of spots where they died." He produced a map of Bandera County and pointed to two Xs, looking pleased with himself. "This is where Bertha found them."

"Fantastic. Do you think we can find it?"

"Do you think you can avoid poison ivy?" He grinned.

Twenty-Nine

We drove into Bandera on Main Street and continued past Texarita's Grill and Cantina. Realistic looking cowboys still lounged on the roof and gazed down at motorcycles and cars parked in front of the establishment.

"I never expected to see motorcycle riders hanging out with Texas cowboys," I said.

We stayed on Highway 16 through town. After we left town and crossed Highway 173, we saw the entrance to the BVSBar Ranch ahead of us in the distance. Before we reached the ranch entrance, we turned south on a country road and continued for about a quarter mile. A fence paralleled us on the right.

"I think that fence marks the eastern boundary of the ranch," he said. When the fence line and the road we were on turned right, he stopped the car and looked at the map. "If we veer right and follow the direction of the fence, we should be driving along the ranch's southern border."

We had driven about three-fourths of a mile when the fence stopped at a corner and angled north. He slowed the car, turned right and pointed to the property inside the fence. "I think that's where they died, somewhere in this remote southwest corner of the ranch."

He began looking for a place to pull off the road. He found an area where tall whitebrush would help hide the car and rolled to a stop. The small amount of rain had made the shrub blossom with white and violet-tinged flowers. As I eased out of Sam's Caprice, I smelled the vanilla scent. We looked around and didn't see a soul.

He checked the map. "I'm pretty sure these corner fences border BVSBar property. This has to be the place. I'll go first." He walked through mesquite, tarbush and bluestem toward the fence, watching for snakes and poison ivy. He found a section of the five-strand barbed wire fence where the bottom wire was loose and motioned me to follow.

I picked my way through the brush, careful where I stepped, and joined him at the fence. We looked around and still didn't see anyone. He held up the loose bottom wire so I could crawl underneath it. I flattened my stomach against the dirt and scooted through like a salamander. I had to be sure none of the barbs protruding from the wire above my back scratched my ivy rash. After I wriggled underneath and brushed dirt off the front of my shirt, I held up the strand for Sam to crawl under. He slipped his Glock and cell phone under the fence, then wiggled under the wire.

We were in a wilderness where only wild animals and livestock might come to graze. If Max and Billy Sue Vernon had come here, no one would have heard their cries for help.

He stood, replaced his pistol and phone and brushed himself off. "If there was a well anywhere near here, there should still be some sign of it."

About ten yards inside the corner from where the fences met, we noticed a cluster of live oaks.

"Look how those trees form a circle," I said. "Beautiful."

"Brush and grasses inside the circle grow taller than the surrounding brush," he said, "from the shade."

One particular patch of plants growing inside the circle of trees caught my attention. Some plants, growing on single stalks, were five feet tall. A foot up each stalk, round notched leaves, succulent like miniature lily pads, branched out. Higher up the stalks, differently shaped serrated leaves branched off the stem. Five-petal flowers popped off in pairs at various intervals.

"So this is where she gets it," I said, pointing at the tall stalks. "That's jewelweed. When Bertha gave me ice cubes made from the plant, I wanted to find out what I was rubbing on myself. I found photos online. Those plants with the greenish-white flowers are jewelweed. It usually grows in moister areas." I thought about the bags of orange cubes in Bertha's freezer. "Bertha must have planted the jewelweed here. She probably didn't want everybody to know she had it."

"Why not?"

"Charlatans boil it with liquid in various concentrations and sell it as a cure for all sorts of skin abrasions. It's a good remedy, but if they don't bother to prepare it correctly, they're selling scam products. Bertha wanted jewelweed to treat the minor cuts and skin abrasions that people get on the ranch, but she must have concluded it was better to keep her stash private. She wanted a place where her jewelweed would thrive, and she could come get it whenever she wanted."

He looked perplexed. "But why would she plant it here? Near where her beloved aunt and uncle died? She apparently hated the idea that some company was drilling on this ranch. Why plant her jewelweed anywhere near the site?"

Why indeed? The trees provided cover from the sun, but there must be similar areas in other parts of the ranch. Maybe we weren't anywhere near the old well.

"Are you sure this is the right location?"

He stepped off the distance from where I stood to the property line at the fence and checked the map. "This looks right."

He walked back to me, and we moved closer to the jewelweed. The area where it grew was completely shaded. Nothing else outside the circle of trees looked as healthy or grew as tall.

Sam studied the area. "Grows in a moist area," he muttered to himself. He searched around until he found a thin, sturdy tree branch about four feet long. He used it to probe through the brush. Then he started prodding the ground around plants that had tall stalks. I inched closer.

He moved from plant to plant. "The ground feels soft. Especially here." He got on his knees and felt around the base of the plants. “It’s damp. I think there’s a water source here somewhere.”

He crawled into the middle of the jewelweed plants and patted the ground. He stopped suddenly and pushed his probe down deep. He dropped one arm into a hole. He withdrew his arm, lifted up his hand and grinned at me. His hand was dripping wet.

“This was a water well,” he said. “They drilled for water here, not oil. Water’s like gold around here. They call it blue gold.”

He kneeled and reached farther down into the hole. He stuck the tree branch down as far as it would go. “There’s a concrete casing inside the old well. It’s probably an old casing that will have to be replaced, but there’s a lot of water down there.”

“No wonder Bertha didn’t want anybody drilling on this ranch,” I said. “She knew there was no oil here, and she didn’t want anybody to find this well. The paper I saw in her room about drilling a well must have been papers referring to re-drilling this water well.”

“Demand for water grows daily,” he said. “Bertha might have something here as valuable as oil.”

“And drilling for water is a lot cleaner than drilling for oil.”

“This makes me understand Bertha better,” he said. “This well is her insurance policy. She does everything she can to make the BVSBar succeed as a guest ranch. But whether the venture succeeds or fails, she has this natural water source.”

“She has to save enough money to re-drill the well,” I said. “I guess that’s why she works so hard to make the ranch succeed. Plus, I think she loves managing the dude ranch.”

I thought about the conversation I overheard between Bertha and Herb. “I wonder why Herb thought his parents were drilling for oil on the ranch when he was growing up?”

“How old was he then?”

“Between seven and ten, I think. He must have heard his parents discussing the well, saw the tall tower the drillers used, and thought they were drilling an oil well. A young child who’d never seen either kind of drilling equipment wouldn’t know the difference.”

"No, he probably wouldn't," Sam said.

"The Vernons must have worried about survival during those drought years. They probably never thought it important to explain to their child the details of what they were doing. When Herb was twelve, Maria told me they sent him to school in San Antonio, and he was glad to go. Shortly after he left, the well dried up. Whatever he knew about it didn't matter. I do wonder," I said, "now that Bertha and Herb are adults, why she never bothered to tell Herb there never was an oil well."

"From what you've told me, Bertha wants Herb to go away and leave her alone. She doesn't want him poking around in her business. He apparently has no claim to the executive rights anyway."

"True. Since Bertha's always been the one who cared about the ranch and worked the ranch, maybe she enjoys watching Herb ooze with greed when he contemplates getting money from a nonexistent oil well."

He nodded. "Before they died, the Vernons must have discovered that their natural source of water had returned. They might have told Bertha."

"Maybe the Vernons' attorney knows about this well."

He looked at his watch. "It's two o'clock. I have his name in the car. If he'll see us, we have time to drive back to San Antonio."

Thirty

After groveling under a barbed wire fence in ranch clothes, I felt too grubby to ascend twenty-five floors above downtown San Antonio in a wood-paneled elevator to enter a plush law office. That's where Marshall Darren, Max and Billy Sue Vernon's attorney, worked. We were glad he could see us.

We hoped he could shed light on what had happened with the water well and why the Vernons died. He might even provide crucial information as to why somebody might have wanted to attack Vicki Landsdale.

On our drive back to San Antonio, Sam brought Marshall Darren up to date by phone. He told Darren he was an SAPD detective vacationing at the BVSBar dude ranch incognito when Vicki Landsdale had her "accident." He related all we knew about the Vernons' untimely deaths, about Herb and Bertha, and that we had discovered the water well.

We washed our hands and faces in the building bathrooms before entering his office. Darren invited us in, and we shook hands. Marshall Darren, in his sixties, looked very prosperous in his silk suit. His maroon tie matched the carpet as well as the matting around photographs of his thoroughbred horses. His wavy gray hair complemented steel blue eyes that were undoubtedly perceptive.

"Thanks for seeing us on short notice," Sam said.

"I'm glad I'm available," Darren said. "Please, sit down. Max and Billy Sue were fine people."

"We understand the Vernons came to see you the day before they died," Sam said.

"Yes. Actually, they had called me the day prior to coming to my office. Driving over the ranch, they discovered that the well they drilled during the 1950s' drought, that had been dry for years, was brimming with water again. They wanted me to file a permit immediately to re-drill the well. And they wanted me to change their wills. They originally left everything to each other, then to Herb."

We were naturally curious about their wills, but first I wanted to know more about the Vernons' history.

"Could you tell us more about the time when they originally drilled the well?" I asked.

"Of course. Max and Billy Sue, high school sweethearts, married in 1953 at age twenty and moved to the ranch that Max's father owned. Their son Herb was born that year. The Vernons had a few cows and sheep, but the 1950s drought was well underway. The Medina River ran on the north side of the ranch but it finally ran dry. As the drought continued, it was obvious their livestock wouldn't survive. Without a reliable water supply, the Vernons couldn't even buy seed and fertilizer to plant crops. Most Hill Country soil isn't rich enough to farm anyway. Like so many others, the Vernons were desperate. Little Herb grew up in the midst of hardships caused by the drought. To this day, the ranch means hardship to Herb."

"We've heard he rarely returns to the ranch. I guess that explains it," Sam said.

"Yes. During the drought," Darren continued, "center pivot irrigation systems were being developed, but the Vernons could never afford irrigation. Under the rule of capture, however, passed by the Texas legislature in 1904, a landowner owned rights to groundwater under his land.

"Max's father had saved up some money. By the time Herb was six, in 1959, the family had scraped up enough money to hire a company to drill a water well on the ranch. The Vernons plunged everything they had into paying for that well. The company used a big tall drilling rig and drilled a cable-tool well as deep as they could—close to 1000 feet."

I turned to Sam.

"That tall drilling rig must have been the rig Herb saw," I said. "He thought they were drilling for oil."

Sam nodded.

"I imagine that's exactly what he thought," Darren said. "After the Vernons died, and I read their wills giving Bertha the ranch, Herb didn't have much to say to me. Herb did call not too long ago, though. He said that since he owned half the minerals, he wanted me to find some oil company to drill on the ranch. I told him there wasn't any oil under that ranch, but I don't think he believed me."

"So until you read their wills, Herb didn't know the Vernons had given the ranch to Bertha instead of to him?" I asked.

"As executor, I wasn't permitted to tell Herb or Bertha the couple had changed their wills. The Vernons thought that Bertha, having lived and worked on the ranch, would preserve it. They thought Herb would let it deteriorate and sell it. The Vernons said they would tell Bertha and Herb that they changed their wills at the appropriate time."

"Do you think the Vernons told them before they died?" I asked.

"I can't be positive, but from Herb and Bertha's reactions when I read the will, I don't believe either one previously knew about the changes."

"What happened to the water well?" Sam asked.

"It ran fine for several years and produced enough water to get the Vernons out of their financial hole. They could grow their own food and feed livestock. They bought Angora goats, and with water to sustain grasses and shrubs, the herd increased. The Vernons made a good living from sheering the mohair fleece off their goats twice a year.

"Hill County people started taking in visitors, so that's what the Vernons did. With the Medina River running through part of the ranch, the Vernons' eighteen hundred acres was the perfect setting for a dude ranch. Old man Vernon helped Max build the lodge and the cabins up until the time he died.

"When Billy Sue's brother and his wife died in a plane crash, Billy Sue and Max took in Billy Sue's niece, Bertha Sampson. From then on, Bertha helped the Vernons run the dude ranch. The Vernons legally adopted her. They had quite a spread and enough water to support it. Herb never cared about the ranch. They sent him to school in San Antonio when he was twelve. Right after that, the well dried up again. That was 1965."

"What made the well dry up?" I asked.

"The Vernons didn't know it when they started, but the company had drilled into the Trinity Aquifer. They were close to the Edwards-Trinity Plateau, but the amount of available water was more variable in the Trinity Aquifer than in the Edwards. Drilling a well in the Trinity was a hit-or-miss proposition. When the drought led so many people to drill wells and develop irrigation systems, the underground aquifers fell. When the water table fell, water went farther underground, and the Vernons' well went dry."

"By that time, the dude ranch had become profitable?" I asked.

"Yes," Darren said, "The Vernons held out as long as they could without well water. Then they obtained another permit to drill a hand well."

"Did Herb start to enjoy coming home?" I asked.

"He came home on holidays during high school. He started college, but he bummed around, didn't learn much and didn't finish. He got odd jobs and continued playing around. He came to the ranch periodically, usually when he wanted money."

"So when the Vernons called you in 1992," Sam said, "they had just driven over the ranch and discovered that their old well was producing water again?"

"Yes. The years 1991 and '92 were terrible drought years for many Texans, but there were sporadic spring rains, and the aquifers recharged. The Vernons wanted me to file an application immediately with Springhills Water Management District, which managed groundwater resources in Bandera County, so they could re-drill their Trinity well."

Sam said, "Springshills later became the Bandera County River Authority and Groundwater District?"

"That's right. As developers built more houses, and water became scarcer, various water districts were formed. Each district had its own rules for landowners to access groundwater. Max and Billy Sue had heard scuttlebutt the Texas legislature was about to pass a bill limiting water that could be pumped from the Edwards Aquifer. So the Vernons were even more eager to obtain a permit to re-drill their Trinity well. Sure enough, in 1993, the legislature gave the Edwards Aquifer Authority power to allocate the amount of groundwater users could pump from the aquifer for irrigation, industrial use, livestock and by land owners."

"Did the Vernons get their application approved?" Sam asked.

"Yes. When they came to my office the day after I spoke with them, we had already obtained the application forms to drill their well. They filled them out, signed them, faxed them back and mailed hard copies. When I inventoried their house in the weeks after they died, I found the permit in their mail allowing them to re-drill the well."

"Surely Bertha and Herb looked through their mail. I'm surprised they didn't find the permit," I said.

"They might have seen the envelope from Springhills Water District, but they wouldn't have thought it important," Darren said. "I told Herb and Bertha I'd take care of mail that looked like bills to be paid. I didn't think Herb would bother to pay them, and I didn't want Bertha to get behind on some obligation and lose the ranch. I knew I needed to take possession of that drilling permit to protect Bertha."

"How sad the Vernons never got to enjoy their well again." I thought I might as well ask Darren the question that had been uppermost on my mind. "Why do you think the Vernons died?"

Before he answered, Marshall Darren took a deep breath and exhaled. "This is just conjecture, you understand. After we completed the application for their drilling permit and made changes they wanted to their wills, it was late when they left for the ranch. The next day, Bertha and Maria said the Vernons announced mid-morning they were going on a treasure hunt. They took sandwiches for lunch, and water. In their excitement, they probably didn't take enough water. When they got to the site, the water table had dropped, and the well had gone dry again."

He sighed. "That well was a sign of life to them. They put hard work and money into the well, and it had saved them. Now, when they thought the water was there for them again, it was gone." He exhaled again. "They were probably exhausted from the activity and excitement of the previous two days. We found out later their Jeep was out of gasoline."

Before Darren continued, he turned his chair around and looked out the window behind his desk. In his mind's eye, I thought he could see the Vernons sitting in their Jeep by their well, in the middle of nowhere. "I wouldn't be surprised," he said, still looking out the window, "if they sat there in that open Jeep and shed tears over that dry well. The time grew later, and the sun grew hotter. My guess is that by the time they gathered themselves together, realized they were out of gas and started to walk home, they were already dehydrated and were stricken by heat stroke. This time, their well couldn't save them." He swiveled back around, sighed and leaned back in his chair.

The three of us sat very still. I had to brush tears from my eyes. The fortunes of life and death were so ironic. So unpredictable.

"Well," Sam said, rising to his feet. "You've explained a lot. We really appreciate the time you've given us."

"Thank you, Mr. Darren," I said. "The Vernons were lucky to have a friend like you."

"Thank you," he said.

Sam and I stood, shook his hand and turned to go.

Sam whirled back around.

"One more thing about the Vernons' wills," he said. "You were able to change them that same day?"

"Yes. When I talked to them on the phone the day before," Darren said, "I told them to make notes on changes they wanted. They would each be writing a new will in my office. Their requests were simple. Each one wanted the surviving spouse to receive everything they owned. If they died in a common disaster, the ranch, with executive rights and half the mineral interests, would go to their niece, Bertha Sampson. Their son Herb would receive an annual stipend of ten percent of the net profit from the ranch, if there was any, plus the other half of the mineral interests. If the ranch made more than $150,000 net profit in a given year, Herb would receive fifteen percent. When the Vernons came to my office the day after we spoke, my secretary and I witnessed each one writing a holographic codicil to their will. They wrote down the changes they wanted, affirmed the other terms of their existing wills and signed the codicils."

"Their new wills were legal and would withstand a challenge?" Sam asked.

"Since my secretary and I both witnessed the couple making holographic codicils to their wills, and since the Vernons were of sound mind, their wills would be hard to challenge in court."

"I see. Thank you again," Sam said.

We left Darren's office and found our car. Sam maneuvered from IH 35 through downtown San Antonio to IH 10. We headed northwest, back to the Hill Country.

Thirty-One

We drove in silence. I pictured Max and Billy Sue sitting in that yellow Jeep under the broiling Texas sun, expecting another extended drought while they stared at their dried-up well.

"How hopeless and miserable the Vernons must have felt when they saw that well," I said.

"Yes. Droughts are part of life in Texas, one of the worst parts. I read a lot about the weather before I moved back here from Chicago."

"I didn't know you were originally from Texas."

"My dad was a farmer in Marlin, south of Austin."

"Could droughts be due to climate change?"

"If they are, the climate has been changing for a long, long time. Droughts have been recorded in Texas since Spaniards explored the area in the 1500s."

"How long does an area have to go without rain before they call it a drought?"

"Weather scientists divided Texas into ten geographical areas. If any area receives less than seventy-five percent of its average rainfall in a year, drought occurs. Back in 1756, a Central Texas drought dried up the San Gabriel River, forcing missionaries and Indians to abandon their settlement. Each decade since has been marked by at least one period of severe drought. For a hundred years ending in 1992, every area had ten to seventeen drought years. The Edwards Plateau area, which covers the Hill Country, had the most—seventeen years. During the same period, nearly the entire western half of the United States suffered severe to extreme drought ten to fifteen percent of the time."

"Didn't Marshall Darren say drought occurred in the 1950s, when the Vernons first drilled their well?" I said.

"Yes, 1949 to 1957 were some of the worst years on record. By 1951, drought covered nearly all the state. By the next year, the water shortage was critical. There were a few spring rains in north Texas in 1953, but the drought grew worse from 1954 to 1956. Of 254 counties in Texas, 244 were declared federal drought disaster areas."

I looked outside at the sky. The sun shone bright and hot as though the thunderstorm had never happened.

"Soaking spring rains in 1956 finally began to end the catastrophic drought," he said, "It was 1957 before the state was considered normal. Now, we have improved methods for using and conserving water. But with more and more people needing water, the struggle is far from over."

"How do you remember all those statistics?" I asked.

"I was born in 1951. Like Herb Vernon, I watched my dad pray for rain so he could make a living. I started studying the history of rainfall in Texas, and I didn't want to depend on the amount of rainfall for my survival. What I experienced personally and what I learned prompted me to go to college and law school."

"Wasn't a play called *The Rainmaker* based on the drought?" I said. Since Sam had been an English major, I thought he'd know.

"The play opened on Broadway in 1954. Richard Nash wrote it after he traveled through drought-stricken Texas in the early '50s."

I nodded. We reached the town of Boerne and turned left onto Highway 46. In a few more miles, we'd be traveling through Bandera and back to the ranch with greater appreciation for what the Vernons withstood to save the BVSBar. We still had a lot of unanswered questions.

I looked over at Sam. "Darren thought Herb and Bertha didn't know the Vernons had changed their wills," I said. "Do you think he's right?"

"He based his opinion on their reactions when he read the will aloud."

"That sounds like a lawyerly answer. Suppose Herb had called the ranch a couple of days earlier and learned the Vernons were going to San Antonio on business. What if he arrived the night they returned home? Maybe he hit hard times, needed money, and the blonde bimbo he married prodded him to find out what was going on."

Sam expanded the idea. "In their excitement," he said, "Max and Billy Sue could have been giggling about the old well. Maybe Herb overheard them. He probably thought they were discussing an oil well."

"Yes," I said, "and if he could bump off the Vernons and manage to implicate Bertha, he'd own the ranch and all the minerals. He'd be rich." I contemplated whether Herb was capable of killing his parents and how he might have done it.

He was apparently thinking the same thing. "Herb probably knew both his parents took diuretics."

"I saw several bottles of diuretics in Bertha's medicine cabinet. It would have been easy enough for Herb to slip into her room, grab a few pills and dissolve them in his parents' thermoses the next morning before he left. Maria was used to Herb popping in at odd times. He might have put diuretics in their thermoses right under Maria's nose."

"Okay," he said. "Then he'd have to figure out how to implicate Bertha. He knew Bertha would probably be the one to find them. And he was right. He'd be far away when Bertha found their bodies. But when the investigation showed no foul play, Bertha was no longer a suspect." He hesitated and glanced over at me. "Bertha could have been the one to slip diuretics into their thermoses."

We grew quiet.

His comment reminded me of something else that was bothering me.

"Vicki said the Vernons' wills specified Bertha couldn't sell the ranch to a developer. She said Bertha wouldn't do that anyway, but I wish I'd asked Darren if that stipulation was true. He didn't mention any such provision in the Vernons' wills."

"I'll call Darren tomorrow and ask him about it."

I loved the way Sam and I worked together. Cooperation was more satisfying than being sneaky.

Thirty-Two

I had just spotted the main gate when Sam pulled the car over to the side of the road. He turned toward me and gently held my shoulders with both hands. "Don't forget what you promised."

My heart started pounding. I tried to recall what I'd promised.

He looked at me intently. "We're pretty sure Vicki's fall wasn't accidental. We know people who don't like her. She rejected two men who chased her, and we're not sure about her relationship with the others. While the clues you found on the trail don't prove anything yet, they provide good circumstantial evidence that somebody contrived to make Vicki's horse throw her."

He stopped talking while I considered what he said.

He resumed speaking, his tone more intense. "Those items didn't just happen to land where Vicki fell. Herb Vernon might think Bertha confided information to Vicki to implicate him in his parents' deaths. I believe there's a killer at this ranch. Don't cross any of these people. Don't follow them or pry in their business."

Sam came close to reading my mind. I'd been contemplating ways to flush out Vicki's attacker.

"A person who could kill a young girl like that is pure evil." He enveloped me in a hug. "You're precious to me, Aggie. I don't want to lose you."

My brain fuzzed.

Was I precious as part of his happy memories from Chicago? Was he beginning to care just for me? Did I care which one it was? It was delicious being in his arms.

He cradled my face in his hands and looked into my eyes. I hoped they were less squinty than Wo Fat's. My eyes changed from green to blue depending on what I wore, the same way Sam's daughter Lee's eyes used to change color. It seemed as though he stared at my eyes for eons. What did he see?

I slipped my face from his hands and turned to look out the front window. "I need time to think before we go back to the ranch."

"All right." He heaved an exasperated sigh. Then he settled back in the seat and closed his eyes.

I remembered the time when we lived in the same apartment building in Chicago, Sam and Katy Vanderhoven and me. We were young, struggling, working our way up. Sam and Katy had met in Chicago, and she had put him through law school. When he decided he'd rather catch criminals than yap about them, he joined the FBI. Then he joined Chicago PD. That's when I met him and Katy, and we became fast friends.

When Lester came into the bank, and I started dating him, we made a foursome. I wasn't sure how well Katy and Sam liked Lester, but they included him. By the time Lester and I fell in love and decided to marry, Sam had reached detective grade. He and Katy were talking about adopting a baby.

Lester said they were foolish to want children. He never wanted to be tied down. The trouble was, I was pregnant. I didn't tell Lester at first. I told Katy and made her promise not to tell Sam.

When I finally told Lester, he bolted.

I was barely nineteen, with no family, no money, and a new, tenuous job as a bank teller. How could I care for a child? I'd have to rear my son or daughter on welfare. Back then, companies didn't offer childcare at work.

I knew the Vanderhovens were the best parents my baby could ever have.

Katy and I talked and talked. I wanted her and Sam to rear my child. But there was one condition: I made Katy promise that Sam would never know I was the baby's mother.

Katy's doctor and lawyer agreed to help Katy and me arrange the birth and adoption details to keep them secret. I managed to get myself transferred to a branch bank in the suburbs early in my pregnancy and work there until after my daughter was born.

The day I had my baby, Katy's doctor called her and Sam. He told them he just delivered a beautiful baby girl who needed a good home. Were they interested? Fortunately, the baby didn't look like me.

Katy and Sam were ecstatic. They welcomed the baby into their home and named her Lee.

Six months after Lee's birth, I transferred back to the main bank in Chicago and watched Sam and Katy raise their beautiful daughter without interference from me. I was her "Aunt Aggie."

I glanced over at Sam. Once before I thought he suspected that, because of our distinctive eyes, Lee could be my daughter. But Lee's other features were different from mine.

I looked over again. He had drifted against the window and started snoring. I was glad to have time to think.

Years later, when Katy and Lee died in the auto accident, Sam's life was shattered. I was devastated. But Sam and I had to grieve separately. If he ever found out I'd deceived him...

I sat still a few more minutes and listened to him snore. Then I touched his arm to wake him. He looked over with sleepy eyes and studied my face. He pulled me over, raised my chin and kissed me, even though I looked like Wo Fat. His kiss wasn't urgent. It was a you-are-dear-to-me kiss.

When he kissed me after we solved the other murder case, I wasn't sure if his kisses came from affection or from relief that I didn't get us both killed.

He put his arm around me. I snuggled into his side and put my head on his shoulder. We were content to sit quietly and recover from a long day.

Before I kissed Sam, I'd only kissed Lester. That was twenty years ago. But I did know the difference in kisses. Lester was selfish and clumsy—a young fool bent on chalking up belt notches.

Eighteen years old and happily naïve, I didn't realize what a clod he was until after he left. Then I was so emotionally distraught at being used and jilted that the thought of spending time with another man was downright painful. My post-Lester sex life was...stunted.

After Sam and Katy adopted Lee, I stayed busy working long days, climbing my way up to bank vice-president and studying at night. Years passed before I realized I was keeping other men at arm's length because I loved Sam. He and Katy were busy rearing their daughter. Until...

Sam drew me closer and wrapped me in a hug.

With his heart still vulnerable, I knew he needed me as a friend. I needed him for my life. But it was way too early to stake that claim.

Smoothing his cheek with my hand, I raised my lips to his. It occurred to me I might be missing an opportunity. I pressed myself against him. We kissed with more urgency. I could try to seduce him. I'd get things moving, and he'd take it from there.

As we clung to each other, an unwelcome thought flicked across my mind. Seducing him might not be the best way to initiate a sustainable relationship. Sam had integrity. And I probably had poison ivy sap on my lips.

After twenty celibate years, I shouldn't leap on Sam like a crazed banshee. He already questioned most of my actions.

If I succeeded in seducing him, I'd be getting only part of the man I knew was there. That approach wouldn't be fair to either of us. Not as the beginning of a long-term commitment.

Our relationship wasn't cemented enough for me to reveal that I was Lee's birth mother. I lacked courage. Plus, the backs of my thighs itched. Plus, we were awfully close to the main gate.

I pulled back, peered into his eyes and touched his cheek. I might as well face it: even if we could be totally truthful about the past, neither of us was the type to enjoy casual sex. We had both endured too much reality to think sex cured everything. I was generally known for plunging into action, not for self-control. Using self-discipline felt different. Controlling my emotions felt good. I was proud of myself.

He scowled at me, his expression a mix of anger and confusion.

"I know you're worried about our safety, Sam. Meredith and I will be careful, I promise. I know if Vicki dies, you can solve her murder. But you need to be careful, too. What would Meredith and I do without you?"

That jarred him back to our immediate problem. He was back in charge. Once a detective, always a detective. He nodded somberly and squeezed my hand. He checked for traffic, pulled back onto the road and aimed for the ranch entrance.

I inhaled and let out a sigh. We had time. Plenty of time. Meanwhile, we had crimes to solve.

Thirty-Three

As we drove through the gate, Sam looked at his watch. "We have a couple of hours before dinner. You said Wayne Rickoff spent time at a VA hospital? Let's see if he's at the firing range."

"Good idea." While I pictured the bleeding elk Rickoff had shot, Sam and I walked toward the range. We heard the veteran blasting away.

We sat and watched him shoot from an observation bench until he noticed us and walked in our direction.

"You're really a good shot," Sam told him, producing a friendly smile.

"Yeah." Rickoff smirked. I wished he'd put down his gun. "That was one thing about being rehabbed up there," he said. "That north country's just lousy with them trophy elk."

"Sounds like Wisconsin. I hunted up there with a friend a couple of times. It was only five hours from my home in Chicago."

"Sure 'nuf?" He leaned conspiratorially toward Sam. "After I got out of the VA hospital, I stuck around just for the hunting. Had a buddy who worked on a private ranch... said we should hunt up in the Northwoods."

Before he could repeat the details of his bloody, unlawful hunt, Sam interrupted. "Were you ever at that VA hospital in Milwaukee? Zablocki? Something like that?"

"Yeah. Zablocki Medical Center. It's an okay place. They had a lotta entertainment for vets."

"Aren't there a lot of horse shows and rodeos around there?"

Rickoff stepped back. His face turned sour. He gave us a hard look. "Yeah," he said. "Among other things." He whirled around, still holding his gun, and stomped back to the firing area. "I gotta practice before dinner."

"See you at the campfire, Wayne." I waved at his back but didn't expect an answer.

"That's one angry man," Sam said.

When we were far enough from the shooting range, Sam slipped into the brush and clicked open his cell phone. I dawdled around on the road picking up rocks and pretending to find them fascinating in case somebody joined us.

Sam emerged from the thicket. "I called the Landsdales. They're in Vicki's room. She's still unconscious. Marcia was crying in the background, and Steve could hardly talk. He confirmed that the Zablocki VA Medical Center was where Vicki went with her no-good boyfriend to pick up vets and take them to rodeos."

I remembered how Vicki stared at the vet before leaving the dining hall. "I wonder if Wayne Rickoff and Vicki recognized each other."

"Could be." Sam fingered his gun. "You need to stay away from the firing range. That man is dangerous. And Aggie..."

"Yes?"

"Try to stay out of trouble. At least until dinner. I'm going to go clean up. See you at the lodge."

My eyes narrowed. "I'll go find Meredith," I replied sweetly. "She went horseback riding this morning. We'll see you later."

If I concocted a plan, I'd probably have to postpone it until after dinner anyway. In the meantime, I thought I might be able to learn something.

Thirty-Four

Once Sam was out of sight, I doubled back toward the shooting range. I wasn't going to put myself in danger by letting Rickoff see me. I was just curious about what he'd do next. Sam's admonishment made me eager to snoop before dinner. I walked close to the brush in case I had to scoot into the thicket and hide. I was pretty far from the range, but I spotted Rickoff.

The shooting stopped. I froze and angled deeper into dense growth. Peeking through mesquite, I saw Rickoff walk away from the practice area and enter a storage building near his cabin. He came out without his gun, thank goodness.

Instead of turning right to enter his cabin, he started heading toward the lodge. I stayed hidden in the bushes. When he was almost to the lodge, he took a sharp right on to the trail that ran around the side to the back of the building. I knew there was a trail behind the lodge, but I'd never been on it. I strolled casually down the main road in front of the lodge. As soon as I passed the building, I hid in the brush again. Rickoff reappeared on the main trail, then veered right to cut though low brush. He was walking in the general direction of Sunny Barlow's cabin. Naturally, I followed.

I was doing a good job of hanging back and walking soundlessly like an Indian until I stepped on a twig. Hopefully, Rickoff was too deaf from shooting to hear me. I crouched down and listened, still as a stump. My heart thumped. Rickoff didn't break stride and was definitely headed toward Sunny's cabin. I bent over and walked on all fours to make sure I didn't inadvertently step on crackling undergrowth. I probably looked like a grubby, prehistoric mammal.

Moving in a wide swath, I circled around to the back of Sunny's cabin. By the time I got there, I'd managed to tear my sleeves and scratch my arms. My hands quivered from supporting my weight.

Sunny's windows were open. He was apparently taking advantage of fresh air after the storm. When I heard Rickoff knock on his front door, I skittered closer to the back of the cabin to eavesdrop.

As soon as Sunny opened the door, Wayne accosted him.

"You followed me to this dude ranch, didn't you? You wanted to get even for when I attacked you at the rodeo."

"Hold on, Rickoff."

"I saw Vicki Landsdale recognize me. She must've told you I was the vet who clobbered you. Are you trying to send me back to that damn hospital?"

"Nah, Wayne. You're way off. But you're right that Vicki saw you attack me when I clowned at the rodeo. I already knew it was you. I recognized you when I first came here—even before you shaved off your beard. I admit I kept hoping you might decide to work somewhere else, but I'm way past holding a grudge. I understood why you vet guys lash out. By the time you whacked me, I'd grown up. I wasn't a teenager anymore."

They grew silent.

Why didn't one of them say something? The silence was creepy. Did Rickoff have a gun hidden on him?

I didn't know how much longer I could stand there without making a sound. I finally heard Rickoff's gruff baritone.

"Okay, Barlow. If you say so. But I'll tell you one thing: don't start getting any ideas, or you'll wish you hadn't. I'm damn sure not going back to that hospital."

"No problem, Rickoff. It was a long, long time ago."

"Yeah." When I heard Rickoff shuffle off, I waited for Sunny to shut the door and used the sound to muffle my sprint back to the brush. I meandered in a wide circle back to the lodge. When I got near the building, I rolled my sleeves down to cover my scratches and sauntered around from the back to the far side, trying to act like I was out for a casual stroll. When I was sure there was nobody around, I hustled back to the main road to our cabin to clean up.

Rickoff must have scarred Sunny's face. Had Sunny really forgiven him, or was he just playing it cool until he found the right time to get even?

Were we going to have another catastrophe at the BVSBar? I doubted Sunny could shoot nearly as well as Rickoff. I was halfway to the cabin before my heartbeat returned to normal.

Thirty-Five

When I got to our cabin, Meredith was dressed for dinner and bursting to tell me what she learned at the stable. When she noticed my grubby shirt and scratches, I told her not to worry; I'd walked through some brush and had another long-sleeved shirt to wear.

"I'm dying to hear what you learned this morning," I told her. "Will you wait for Sam while I clean up and answer letters to Dear Aggie? Then you can tell Sam and me both on our way to the lodge."

"Sure," she said, and headed for the bench under the oak tree to wait for Sam.

I set a record freshening up for dinner and plopped down at my computer to research Wayne Rickoff's service records, especially his medical history. What if he'd been discharged for anger issues? Were we sitting on a time bomb?

I searched Ask Jeeves for the National Archives and Veterans Service. Veterans and next of kin could obtain free copies of a record of their military service called Report of Separation to obtain post-service employment or verify their qualification for military benefits and retirement. Even if I could obtain Rickoff's service record, which I couldn't, it apparently contained general information such as duty stations, assignments, training, awards, medals and administrative remarks.

The only revealing data on the report might be disciplinary actions taken against Rickoff, which wouldn't necessarily equate to PTSD anger issues.

I tried the National Personnel Records Center, which stored records of mental health treatment of military retirees. The site looked promising, until I read, “Before sending a request to NPRC, contact the last medical treatment facility to determine if a patient’s records have been retired to the NPRC.”

This was a dead end. The patient protection act, HIPAA, precluded medical facilities from releasing medical information except to veterans and next of kin. NPRC’s information was available to a third person only if the veteran authorized them to receive it. That would never happen. Strike two.

My last option was the Freedom of Information Act. Some military service information could be obtained without the veteran or next of kin’s authorization, like the transcript of a trial if the veteran had been court-martialed.

The information might not relate to a service man’s mental health, but I typed in “Wayne Rickoff.” No record of court-martial. Strike three.

It appeared that Meredith, Sam and I would have to plow through our remaining time at the ranch suspecting and fearing Wayne Rickoff, but knowing little about him. If we left the ranch without learning more, I supposed Sam could share what little we knew with local authorities.

I shut down the laptop and peered outside the cabin door in time to see Sam marching toward Meredith in detective stride.

The girls came out of their cabin, giggling, except for Millie, who still looked pale. Meredith told them to go ahead to the lodge without us.

When I joined Meredith and Sam, his furrowed brow told me our vacation days were coming to an end. “I heard Selma tell George they should leave the ranch,” he said, “that the wild-eyed vet who shoots everything in sight gives her the creeps.”

“I think we agree with Selma on that one,” I said. “I searched online for Rickoff’s service records, but they’re not available to the general public.”

We started walking toward the lodge.

"Selma said if Vicki could get thrown, she wondered how safe the other horses were," he said.

I pictured Marbach, swiveling his rear in position to kick me to kingdom come.

"George agreed that if Vicki died," he said, "guests would scatter like mice. If everybody left, Selma said, at least George wouldn't have to suffer at the dude ranch anymore."

He stopped and frowned. "The funny thing was, just before I left the cabin, I heard George tell Selma to call the Nature Conservancy. She had a friendly conversation with whoever answered. George kept prompting Selma to ask questions. I couldn't hear all they said, but I thought I heard them mention Bertha Sampson."

"That is strange," I said. "Selma's into conservation, but from what I can tell, George rejects the whole concept."

Sam agreed. "Why would George Tensel encourage Selma to discuss Bertha with the conservancy?" We inched toward the lodge comparing notes.

Sam and I dreaded it, but we knew we had to tell Meredith that Vicki might die and that we thought somebody at the ranch had tried to kill her. When Sam told her, she stopped dead still.

"What kind of monster could kill that young girl? Why?"

"That's what we have to find out," he said.

When Meredith asked how we concluded someone caused Vicki's fall, we described the clues I'd found on the trail.

"Animal hair, rope, and wire wouldn't be accidentally lying near where Vicki fell," Sam said. "We think somebody used those items to spook her horse."

I also had to tell Meredith the crime lab scientist said that paint on the rock I found matched Sunny Barlow's face paint.

She was stunned. "Not Sunny..."

I switched the focus back to Rickoff. "Any noise might have spooked Vicki's horse," I said, "like a shot from Rickoff's gun. Vicki told me that when Rickoff was angry about something once, he sighted her for a few seconds through his gun scope."

"I didn't know that," Sam said.

"I forgot to tell you," I said. I decided to reveal I'd had a brief talk with Sunny. "Years ago, Rickoff cut Sunny's face at a Wisconsin rodeo. Sunny said when Vicki accompanied her boyfriend to the rodeo, she witnessed the attack."

Sam gave me a questioning look. "Sunny told you that?" he said.

"He let it slip." I wasn't about to tell Sam I followed Rickoff to Sunny's cabin to eavesdrop.

Instead, I told Meredith how the Landsdales described Vicki's brother Trey and why they sent him to the ranch. "I suspect he has a major drug problem," I said.

"Why would Sunny or Rickoff or brother Trey want to kill Vicki?" Meredith said.

"We don't know that any of them wanted to kill her, only that each one had a connection to her," Sam said.

I didn't mention the note from Vicki I found in Sunny's cabin. I couldn't admit I'd been in there, and I wasn't sure what the note meant.

"We'll catch the bastard," Sam said, "whoever he is." He hesitated. "I called the hospital again this morning," he said. "Vicki's still in a coma."

"Oh, no..." Meredith said.

Sam looked pointedly at Meredith and me. "Don't forget that whoever tried to kill Vicki Landsdale is probably still here. Don't forget to watch your backs."

Trying to absorb everything she just learned, Meredith took a deep breath before she spoke. "I learned a few things at the corral this morning. I was petting Vicki's horse and noticed a mark on its back. I wondered if somebody put a burr under the saddle to make it pitch. When I moved closer to study the sore spot, Ranger Travis slipped up behind me and barked at me to leave the horse alone.

He said the horse was still nervous from the storm, sirens and helicopter and might hurt me. The horse didn't look skittish to me.

I think Ranger wanted to scare me away from investigating anything involving Vicki's fall."

"I noticed earlier," I said, "that when Ranger tried to flirt with Vicki, she gave him the cold shoulder."

Sam shook his head. "I should get you two out of here before you get hurt."

Thirty-Six

I hated hearing Sam talk about leaving. We'd learned so many new facts and needed time to fit the pieces together. We kept walking toward the lodge.

"More happened at the corral," Meredith said. "After Ranger shooed me away from the horse, I saw Monty talking to a cowboy that I'd never seen before. His hat hid most of his face, and his hair hung longer than his chin, so I couldn't see his features.

"He glowered down at Monty," she said. "'I'm riding with you,' he told Monty. They walked into the barn. I ambled closer, petting horses as I went, so I could eavesdrop. I couldn't hear much, except when they talked loud."

"Monty said, 'Ranger's got enough wranglers. He can't hire you.'

'If he don't, you're going back to jail,' the cowboy said.

'Nah. That can't happen...'

'Sure as hell can,' the cowboy said. 'You probly told the boss you just cut a gang member. I heard that kid died. Bet your boss don't know that.'

"Monty looked real worried. When they came out of the barn, I turned my back and pretended to be totally engrossed in my horse. But I could still hear them."

"'Got me a sweet deal here,' Monty said. 'Might be head wrangler someday. I can't go back to that jail.'

"'Then cut me in on your deal,' the guy said. 'If anybody here gets suspicious... get rid of 'em.'"

"They were walking toward me, so I fiddled with my horse's cinch. Monty came over and introduced the cowboy as Currin Dowdy, a guy from his rodeo days. Dowdy looked at the ground. Just then, Selma showed up and said she'd try to ride because she didn't want to get back in the river. Ranger saddled a horse for her that looked like it was asleep, and we mounted.

"Nobody talked during the ride," Meredith said. "Selma was too scared of her horse to say much. Dowdy's a big guy, and he rode right behind Monty the whole way, like he was trying to intimidate him. When we got back, Selma and I dismounted, and Ranger started talking to Monty and the cowboy in low tones. I couldn't hear what they said."

"Sounds like Dowdy and Monty might have been jailbirds together," Sam said. "Monty's hiding information he didn't tell Ranger."

When we neared the lodge, Sam stopped and turned to us. "I think you and Meredith should make some excuse about a sick relative and go back to San Antonio."

She and I exchanged glances.

"If you take us home and come back," I said, "it'll blow your cover. Somebody's bound to figure out you stayed to investigate and will check you out."

"We can help you, Sam," Meredith said. "We can pick up tidbits without the killer having any reason to suspect us."

I loved Meredith's logic. Since we were all famished, she and I had a reprieve, at least through dinner—maybe through the next day—while Sam decided what to do. If I stepped up my investigation, maybe I could flush out the killer before Sam decided we should leave. At the right time, I'd tell him what I learned, and we could work together. I realized my curiosity was trumping my judgment, but we were so close to learning what happened. It might help Vicki.

Hunger and necessity sharpen one's mind. The bud of an idea took shape.

* * *

In the dining hall, everybody shuffled around in silence while Maria put dinner on the serving bar. There wasn't even much chatter in the food line or after everybody sat. Once guests were settled, Bertha stood.

"I know you're all concerned about Vicki. I'm happy to tell you she's recovering."

The group uttered a collective sigh. Sam, Meredith, and I sliced glances at each other.

"Her parents are with her at the hospital in San Antonio. I'm sure we'll find out more details later. Until then, enjoy your dinner."

Bertha was lying to keep guests from leaving the ranch. My imagination raced. Maybe Bertha and Vicki had argued. Vicki discovered something Bertha didn't want her to know about the Vernons' deaths or the water well. In her anger, Bertha spooked Vicki's horse. Bertha couldn't let everyone know how critical the girl was. If Bertha caused Vicki's fall and the girl died, she'd be ruined.

I glanced at the elk positioned high on the wall with his brown eyes surveying the room. If only trophies could talk. I noticed something different about the smaller animals hanging from the ceiling. Were wires holding them the same kind Ranger used for sculptures? The same type of wire I found where Vicki was thrown? I needed to examine those specimens up close.

Nobody seemed sufficiently motivated to move outside to a campfire. Sunny sang a few songs in the lodge dining room, sad songs. It was nearly dark when we left the lodge to return to our cabins. We three kept to ourselves, speculating about Bertha's announcement and how the others had reacted.

With my feet itching like crazy, I crystallized my plan.

After dark, I'd sneak back to the lodge.

Thirty-Seven

When I was sure everyone was asleep, I popped upright and reviewed my plans. My actions might prove dangerous. I didn't want Meredith involved.

I slipped into baggy jeans, tennis shoes and the pigeon vest I'd stuffed under my sheet. The vest had a pocket for my flashlight in case the moonlight wasn't bright enough for me to see clearly. I crept out the door and stood on the stoop, adjusting my eyes to the darkness. The moon was barely visible, but I could see the path to the lodge well enough not to need my light, so I zipped it in my pocket so it wouldn't fall out. I didn't want to attract attention, especially if a murderer was out prowling.

I'd taken a few steps down the path when I heard something whistling. Sliding into shadows at the path's border, I stood stock-still and listened. The sound came from above me. I looked up. High in a tree, a bird with an owl-shaped head trilled a whistle. A Whippoorwill? Exhaling, I inched forward, still moving close to the brush. The sound of unidentified animals scurrying close by propelled me back onto the path.

When I neared the lodge, I stayed on my side of the path, hiding in shadows, my eyes searching in all directions for movement or sound. Fortunately, the outside of the lodge wasn't lighted except for a tall overhead light on a pole behind the building that cast a soft glow.

When I felt safe, I crossed the path and tiptoed up the steps to the lodge. Squinting between the door and frame, I saw the glow of a nightlight. I turned the knob a smidgen and was surprised to find the front door unlocked. Twisting it with painstaking slowness so it wouldn't squeak, I edged the door open and slipped inside. If Bertha was a killer, I doubted she'd be worried about anyone else coming into the lodge. On the other hand, I might find myself trapped in there with her. I made sure the front door didn't lock behind me, in case I needed to escape.

I knew Bertha's bedroom was to the left of the reception desk. I peeked in the room to make sure she was there. She snored like a bear.

Retrieving the flashlight from my pocket, I covered half the glass with my hand before turning it on. On tiptoe, I crept though the dining room toward the kitchen, thankful to be walking on stained concrete that didn't creak. I found a stepstool in the kitchen, hauled it back to the dining hall without making a sound, and set it beneath the pair of suspended bobcats. When I climbed three steps up the stool, I was high enough so that moonlight streaming through the windows lit the creatures well enough for me to see details. I zipped the flashlight back in my pocket.

Both cats had brown and gray fur, but the reddish cast of fur down their backs was most distinctive. Black spots ran through the fur. The larger cat, probably the male, was three feet long and looked like he weighed around thirty-five pounds. The smaller female, about thirty inches long, probably weighed close to thirty pounds. She was twice the size of an average house cat.

I was close to their round pixie-like faces and black-tufted ears. Their "bobbed" tails had black points marking the tips, as though they'd been dipped in ink. I ran my hand from the top of the female's head to the tip on her tail. Her fur was coarse. I expected the white fur that ran under her chin down to her stomach to be soft, but when I rubbed the fur between my fingers, it felt stiff.

I fingered the wire suspending the female cat.

It appeared to be the same kind Ranger used to sculpt his creatures. Several strands of new wire were twisted together for strength, as though somebody had recently re-hung the cat. Was the old wire I'd found on the trail formerly used to hang these cats?

I reached up to re-position the smaller bobcat, making its tail higher. Now it appeared to look directly down toward the dining room. I wondered whether Vicki's attacker would notice.

I studied the larger cat. Its wires were old and rusty.

"What are you doing in here, girl?" Bertha's gravelly voice nearly knocked me off the stool. When I grabbed the wire to steady myself, I cut my hand. She stood flatfooted in long faded pajamas, her hair shooting broom-like from her head. She pinned me with beady eyes.

"I noticed this bobcat at dinner," I stammered, holding my bleeding hand. "I...I think somebody re-hung this one with the kind of sculpture wire Ranger Travis uses."

To my amazement, Bertha folded into the nearest chair and collapsed into tears. I eased down the stepstool and went over to pat her arm with my non-bleeding hand.

"I'm so sorry. What's wrong?" She was in no condition to kill me, at least not yet.

She rose with effort and padded back to the reception desk, where she snatched a tissue and blew her nose. I followed, not too close, making sympathetic sounds.

I grabbed a couple of Kleenexes and pressed them to my wound to stop the bleeding, stuffed a couple more tissues in my pocket and sniffled with Bertha.

She pointed to the row of wire animal sculptures on a shelf behind the reception desk. "See those?" she said. "They're some of Ranger's finest work."

I'd only glanced at them before. "Those really are good," I said. "I didn't know he was so versatile...talented...flexible." Recalling Ranger's hasty exit with Jangles after dinner, I struggled to find the right word.

"I've got more of his work in my bedroom," she said, motioning me to follow.

Pausing at the threshold, I saw wire sculptures lined up like prizes on the shelf above her bed. Front and center among them was a photograph of Bertha when she was young, thin and gorgeous, standing beside Ranger Travis. Amazing.

"That's how I used to look," she said. "Sometimes age sneaks up too fast."

That was a scary thought. I'd work out at the health club the instant we returned to San Antonio and get serious researching the anti-aging properties of telomeres.

"It's a hard job, running a ranch like this by myself. Ranger used to help me. Until Vicki came." I frowned at her. Had she spooked Vicki's horse out of jealousy? She started crying again.

"I didn't hurt Vicki, if that's what you think. We have our disagreements, but her accident means I could lose this ranch. People might be afraid to come here...afraid of the horses...afraid we're careless... whatever. This here ranch is all I've got. It's my home and I love it." She was crying so hard, I began to believe her. She settled down.

"I found out Vicki was about to leave the ranch," she sniffed. "I went into her cabin the other day, just to check things out. I found maps."

"What kinds of maps?"

"Of a bunch of islands somewhere down past Florida."

Vicki's having the same maps of the Caribbean that Sunny had confirmed it. She really intended to go there. She apparently discussed her departure with Sunny, and Bertha found out. Maybe Bertha spooked Vicki's horse so she couldn't leave. Maybe she just wanted to delay Vicki's departure, but the girl's injuries turned out to be serious. Was it possible Bertha didn't know how critical Vicki's injuries were?

Was it conceivable Sam asked EMS, SAPD, the hospital and Vicki's parents to keep her condition quiet long enough for him to investigate at the ranch? Did he conspire with the Bandera sheriff?

Maybe I wasn't the only one keeping secrets.

If the ranch hands knew Vicki was dying, they might figure they were suspects and flee, especially if they had criminal records or histories of mental instability. That would really stymie ranch operations.

It was more likely Bertha knew the truth about Vicki's condition. Even if she caused Vicki's fall, Bertha would try to maintain normality as long as she could.

I knew one thing for sure; I shouldn't contest Bertha's assertion that Vicki was on the mend. It was better for me to feign ignorance and try to calm Bertha.

"Everything's going to be all right," I said. "We can try to find out what happened without upsetting everybody. I'll try to help. I'm sorry I came in here and startled you. Do you have a flashlight I can borrow to see my way back to the cabin?"

"There's a good moon out. You shouldn't have any trouble getting back," she said, "but you can take this one." She sniffled and handed me a flashlight. "I'm glad to have somebody to talk to. I'll see you at breakfast."

When I stepped outside, the moon was brighter. Two Texas toads jumped sideways off the lodge porch. Mexican tree frogs honked in response. Uncomfortable with the noise, I slipped across the path and started down the other side, trying to stay in the shadows. The moonlight made me feel vulnerable. I didn't know whether anyone followed me to the lodge, or who might be outside waiting. I wrapped Bertha's flashlight in Kleenex and held it tightly in case I needed it for a weapon.

Invisible animals scurried close by through the brush. I imagined small creatures—mice, rabbits and squirrels—trying to escape larger ones like raccoons, skunks and coyotes. I preferred to think the javelinas were someplace else. Thinking about critters kept me from contemplating which human nocturnal hunters might be watching.

I heard, "Whoo whoo whoo whoo, whoo whoo!" and froze. When I looked up, a barred owl with a round monkey face and dark eyes stared me down. His yellowish bill stuffed in his circle of neck feathers made him appear all-knowing. I could imagine him thinking, "I know what you're up to, whoo whoo." I read somewhere that the Romans believed barred owls warded off evil spirits. My protector was watching. I felt calmer.

When I finally reached our cabin and slipped in, I put Bertha's flashlight in a plastic bag with the tissue still wrapped around it. If we needed the forensics lab to extract her prints, I would give the flashlight to Sam.

Thirty-Eight

At sunrise, I donned my last clean long-sleeved shirt to cover scratches I incurred sneaking through the brush to Sunny's cabin. I scribbled a note for Meredith saying I'd meet her at the lodge for breakfast and made sure I was the first person to arrive. Scents from the kitchen told me Maria was cooking sausages and biscuits.

Bertha's door was closed. I heard the shower running in her bathroom. In the dining hall, I parked myself at the table near the entrance so I could evaluate everybody's facial expressions as they came in.

From behind a copy of the *Bandera County Courier*, I peeked at the ceiling. My tail-up bobcat was hard to miss. Several people might notice it. Only one, however, would know that whoever re-hung the cat might have connected it with Vicki's fall. Although I didn't completely understand the connection between Vicki and the cat, her attacker would know.

Maria lit candles under warming pans on the serving line. When Bertha emerged from her room, I noticed she'd applied makeup around her bloodshot eyes. With Vicki out of the picture, I wondered if Bertha would make another play for Ranger. For her strategy to work, she'd have to give up a lot of sausages and biscuits.

Bertha was jealous, but I couldn't quite imagine her trying to kill Vicki. Bertha acted tough, but she could cry buckets. She obviously loved the ranch. She indicated she and Ranger were lovers until Vicki showed up. If she had tried to kill Vicki, I doubted she would have revealed her motive to me. Her spooking Vicki's horse could have been accidental. But I couldn't ignore Herb Vernon's implication that Bertha killed his parents to get the ranch. People had killed for less.

Bertha spotted me, walked over to my chair, narrowed her eyes and studied me. "You're here mighty early," she said. She glanced up at the bobcat, put her hands on her hips and rolled her eyes. "Cute. How's your hand?"

"Much better. It's sore, but the bleeding stopped." I had put antibiotic cream on it and covered it with a small Band-Aid. I didn't want somebody to identify the slash as a wire cut.

She called to Maria. "Is everything ready? Here they come."

Ranger and Monty sauntered in. The hanging bobcat caught their eye. Both tried to act like there was nothing unusual about it, but Ranger squinted at the cat a few extra seconds. He might have been wondering if somebody snitched his wire to re-hang the cat. Or he might have re-hung it himself.

When George and Selma Tensel shuffled through the door, she screamed, grabbed George's arm and pointed up at the leering cat. "That wildcat looks like it's going to leap down here and get us."

"Don't be ridiculous, Selma. It's wired up there. And it's dead." He frowned at the ceiling and rubbed his chin. When he glanced around and saw Ranger and Monty, he glared at their backs looking disgusted. He probably thought they strung it up at a crazy angle to get everybody's attention. When he gazed my way, I managed to appear innocent.

River Rat slouched into the room looking hung over. He didn't even glance up. He might be depressed over killing his sister. When the cabin six girls floated in and fluttered over to sit by him, he put his head in his hands. Jangles' red and orange poncho and jangling bracelets probably made his headache worse. When Stoney slapped him on the back, I thought he might become ill. Millie, mouse quiet, patted his hand.

Sunny dragged in with his head drooping. He spotted me. Even though he wore face paint, I couldn't miss his hostile demeanor. By the time he glanced at the ceiling, he had turned his back so I couldn't see his face. He plopped on a chair at a table by himself. The three girls looked at him wistfully. River Rat was probably contemplating how to make them flock to Sunny's table so Rat could eat in peace.

Meredith and Sam came in last. Sam eyed me suspiciously. "Why did you come here so early?"

I gracefully folded one hand over the other, covering my Band-Aid. "I was ravenous. I've been waiting for you two." He gazed around, glanced up and saw the cat. He looked at me again and lifted his eyebrows.

"The bobcat was crooked," I said. "Bertha and I tried to straighten it before breakfast. We didn't do a very good job, did we?"

He leaned over and got in my face. "You were checking the wire, weren't you?"

I didn't blink.

"Is it the same type of wire Ranger uses to sculpt?"

"Yes."

"Is there something else you need to tell me?"

I had to think fast. "Everybody's going on the morning horseback ride," I said. "It might be the only time everybody is together in one place."

"Yeah. That could be a problem." He lowered his voice to a whisper. "Especially if one of them is a killer."

We went through the breakfast line.

As each person finished eating, they'd steal a questioning glance at Bertha.

Finally, she rose from her table.

"I know we're all thinking about Vicki. She's still unconscious, but doctors are hopeful...We have the final event of your stay this morning, the all-ranch picnic trail ride for guests and wranglers. Everybody goes except me and Maria. By the time you return, maybe I'll know more about Vicki's condition. Don't forget your backpacks. Maria is packing lunches in them. You can get ready for the ride and pick up your backpacks here in about an hour. Here's how you put 'em on."

She stuck meaty arms through side loops connected to a lightweight pack. "These packs are real comfortable. They leave your arms free to hold the reins. This clip at the top attaches to the back of your collar so the pack won't fall off when you ride. They're souvenirs of the BVSBar Ranch for you to keep. Designed 'em myself. Enjoy this beautiful morning riding in the Hill Country. I'll see you here at the lodge when you get back."

Meredith pushed her chair back. "I want to secure my hair under a hat before this ride."

I was about to stand when Sam put his hand on my arm.

"I'll be there in just a minute," I told Meredith. "You go on ahead."

Sam leaned toward me. "I called the Vernons' attorney and asked whether their wills precluded Bertha from selling the ranch to developers. He said the Vernons wanted Bertha to keep the ranch intact and thought having underground water would help her keep the property. But he couldn't advise them to specify in their wills that she couldn't sell the ranch. That provision probably wouldn't be enforceable."

I watched everyone leave. I knew they'd stop by their cabins before returning for backpacks. Sam and I had time to talk. Sunny still sat at his table, so we'd have to keep our voices low.

"If the ranch loses money, what can Bertha do?" I asked.

"The Vernons set up a ten-year agreement with the Texas Nature Conservancy. If, during that time, Bertha decides the ranch can't support her, she gives the ranch to the conservancy. The conservancy agreed to pay Bertha enough to support herself and maintain the ranch during her lifetime. When she dies, if she has no heirs, the conservancy gets the ranch. If she has heirs or adopts children, for example, her heirs will own the ranch. If they reach age sixty, they're subject to the same agreement. Darren wasn't sure the courts would uphold that last stipulation."

"So, in effect, Bertha can't ever sell this ranch."

“Not for ten years from the time she inherited it. If she does, the Nature Conservancy would take the position she failed to uphold the Vernons’ agreement, and the conservancy would own the ranch.”

“Bertha’s had the ranch for five years already,” I said. “She has to keep the ranch afloat five more years.”

“Yes. After that, she owns the ranch free and clear, and she can do whatever she wants with it. Darren said there were more details, but we didn’t have time to go into them.”

“Five more years must seem like a long time to Bertha. No wonder she’s desperate. I wonder if the Vernons told her about their arrangement with the conservancy the night before they died.”

“Maybe they told her, and Herb overheard,” he said.

“Maybe that’s why Herb comes here periodically. He knows Bertha’s under stress. So he harasses her to agree to let oil companies drill on the ranch. He figures he and Bertha will both be rich, and she’ll be able to wait out her five years with the conservancy. After that, he probably thinks he can talk Bertha into developing the property,” I said, “and he can weasel himself into the deal.”

“I find it pretty funny that Herb is pressing Bertha to let somebody drill,” Sam said, “since there’s no oil here. I hope he doesn’t decide to come harass Bertha while we’re away on this trail ride.”

“I’d better tell Maria to stick close to Bertha,” I said. I remembered sensing rage seething in Herb Vernon. He might be capable of more than harassment.

“I’ll swing by the cabin to get my Glock. I’ll pick up my backpack and meet you and Meredith at the stables in about an hour.” He rose and marched off.

I glanced at Sunny still slouching at his table alone. I wanted to talk to him before the ride, but I had to alert Maria. I ran to the kitchen to make sure she and Bertha would be together while everybody else went on the trail ride.

Thirty-Nine

"Is Señora Bertha in danger?" Maria asked, her eyes huge.

"I don't think so. With everybody else gone, it's just a good idea for you two to stick together."

"Something happened, Señora," she told me in Spanish. "Last night, when everybody left after dinner, Ms. Bertha was alone in the dining room."

"Yes?"

"Señor Tensel came in."

"George Tensel?"

"Sí. I was in the kitchen so I listened. He told Ms. Bertha he wanted to buy this ranch. I heard him. She said it wasn't for sale."

"'You'll have to sell eventually,' he said. "'I know the place is losing money. Wait until Vicki Landsdale dies. Nobody's going to come here after that. It's just a matter of time. I can wait.' He looked so evil. She yelled at Señor Tensel to get out. He was angry and sneered at Ms. Bertha. Then he left."

"Thank you for telling me, Maria. George Tensel is going with us on the horseback ride. I don't think he'll come back here any time soon. Herb Vernon might come see Ms. Bertha while we're gone, though. He drops in at unexpected times, doesn't he?"

"Sí, Señora."

"Do you have a gun in here?"

"Sí, Señora. And I know how to shoot it. I grew up on a ranch."

"Okay, good. Put bullets in the gun. If Herb Vernon or anybody else comes in here and starts yelling at you or at Bertha, you get that gun, go to that window over the sink, hold the gun out the window and shoot straight up. We'll hear it, we'll know it's you, and we'll come as fast as we can."

"Esta bien, Señora." She nodded with resolve. "Now I've got to finish these." She continued assembling lunches to put in backpacks.

I thought Maria and Bertha could handle themselves. She had a few backpacks ready, so I grabbed one. I needed to catch Sunny.

Forty

While Sam and I talked, Sunny had left the lodge and was striding toward his cabin. I charged after him and ran up to him, smiling and talking fast before he could shoo me away.

"Sunny, I want to apologize for being in your cabin uninvited. Is your eye okay? I know you'd never hurt Vicki. I have an idea how we can finger the person who did. Can I walk with you to your cabin? I brought you a backpack."

He looked suspicious, but when I mentioned Vicki, he appeared interested. He took the backpack. We kept walking toward his cabin.

"Vicki knew Wayne Rickoff was the vet who attacked you at the Milwaukee rodeo, didn't she?"

He stopped and stared at me. "How'd you know that?"

"I met Vicki's parents at the airport when Sam and I went to San Antonio for supplies. They said she went with her college boyfriend to take vets from the Milwaukee VA hospital to the rodeo. I learned you clowned at that arena and that a vet attacked you."

He looked stunned.

I shrugged. "I went back to college last year and got in the habit of doing research. The hospital keeps a list of where veterans go and who entertains them. I have a friend at the VA hospital who checked the records for me."

I kept talking before he had time to think about exactly how I obtained that information. "Anyway, when I saw that Vicki recognized Wayne Rickoff, I put the pieces together. I also thought about the snake that slithered toward Rickoff when we first toured the ranch. I don't suppose you had something to do with that."

He grinned in spite of himself. "I'm glad the idiot didn't shoot somebody. I like to hassle Rickoff in hopes he'll go someplace else to work." He turned to me. "How'd you know about the snake?"

"Maria started screaming, and Bertha and I found one in the freezer. It was pretty stiff from being cold. Somebody had wired its mouth closed. I remembered the snake at the firing range had something shiny around its mouth. I realized it must have been wire."

He nodded, smiling. "Once you get snakes cold enough, you can wire their mouths shut. It doesn't hurt them, but when they thaw out, they're pretty mad. You can always get them cold again if you want to remove the wire and turn 'em loose. Too bad 'ole Bertha threw that snake out of the freezer. It would have warmed up pretty quick outside. Ready to slither toward ole' Rickoff at the right moment."

"Once a clown, always a clown, huh?"

"I guess so. We think up tricks for our acts. Couldn't do that one with the vets, though, or with kids."

"You keep that cooler in your room for non-poisonous snakes you catch, right? It's not just used for make-up."

He chuckled. "You never know when a thawed, angry snake will come in handy."

"I've got to get ready for the ride," I said. "See you at the corrals?"

He shrugged. "Sure."

The all-ranch ride would be interesting.

Forty-One

I had forty-five minutes before we were to meet at the corrals, and I needed a backpack.

I trotted to the lodge, thinking about George Tensel's greedy mug and cousin Herb's Vernon's menacing scowl. I was glad I had time to check on Bertha and Maria. When I saw that Bertha's Jeep wasn't parked out front, panic closed my throat. I burst into the dining room.

Bertha and Maria sat at a table crying. Bruises around their eyes were dark and puffy.

"What happened?" I screeched.

Blood caked the corner of Bertha's mouth. The women sniffed and moved bags of orange ice cubes to various parts of their faces.

"Who did this to you?" I cried. "Are they here?" I whipped around looking for scoundrels who hurt them.

"Señor Herb," Maria cried.

"My dear cousin," Bertha said.

"Where is he?" I flew through the room and peered in the kitchen. "Where's your gun, Maria?"

"It's still in the drawer, Señora. I couldn't get it." She cried louder.

"Herb didn't get it, either," Bertha said. "He's gone."

"Where is he?" I asked, frantically searching the dining hall.

"Far from here," Bertha said. "Don't worry. He's gone."

I ran to the kitchen, shouting over my shoulder to Maria, "Is the gun still in the drawer under the window?"

"Sí, Señora."

I found the .380 pistol and the bullets and breathed easier. I carried the gun and bullets to the table and sat with Bertha and Maria while I loaded the gun and clicked on the safety. If he came back, I'd be ready. My heartbeat slowed.

"Where is he? Why did he do this?" I looked closer at their injuries. He'd blackened their eyes and split Bertha's lip. He hit both women hard, the bastard.

"After everybody left," Bertha said, "Herb blasted in here. He said I was refusing to drill the oil well so he could never get his part of the minerals. He said I didn't care if he and Bitsy starved. I told him that just wasn't true, that there was no oil on this ranch and never had been. That's when he went ballistic."

"Ay," Maria said. She put her head in her hands.

"He grabbed Maria," Bertha said, "and tried to get her to tell him where the well was. He shook her. She kept saying she didn't know." Maria nodded.

"He didn't believe her. I could tell he was about to hit her, so I ran over and tried to push him away, but he knocked me down and slugged Maria." Maria sniffed. "Then he came after me. When I staggered to my feet, he hit me." Bertha moved the bag of cubes to her other eye and cheekbone.

"Did you try to get the gun, Maria?" I asked.

"No, Señora. I was afraid he'd take it away from me and shoot us."

"He might have, Maria. Then what happened?"

"We were both sitting on the floor, crying," Bertha said. "Herb didn't seem to know what to do next. He asked me again where the well was, so I told him I vaguely remembered it was somewhere in the northwest corner of the ranch."

"Don't you have sheep pens up there?"

"Sure do. Herb's driving around up there somewhere. In my Jeep. He's probably in the middle of a hundred sheep. Looking for that oil well." Bertha laughed and flinched from the pain of moving her face.

"Where's Herb's car?" I asked.

"He yelled at Bitsy to get in their car and drive home."

"We need to call the sheriff," I said.

"I already did," Bertha said. "When I called, the girl who answered said Detective Sam Vanderhoven had already called them to report there might be trouble brewing. The sheriff and deputy are on their way to the ranch." She frowned at me and grimaced again from pain. "Sam is a detective?"

"He came with Meredith and me on vacation and decided not to reveal he was an SAPD detective. But when Vicki's horse threw her, and she was such a good rider, he thought her accident was suspicious."

"He could investigate better if no one knew who he was," Bertha said.

"Exactly."

"Isn't it almost time for the ride?" she said. "When the sheriff comes, I'll tell him where to find Herb. You go on."

"Shouldn't you and Maria be treated by a doctor?"

Bertha looked at Maria. "We've been through worse than this." Maria nodded.

After the Vernons died, these two women ran this ranch by themselves—in the midst of various kinds of two-and-four-legged predators.

"We took Advil," Bertha said. "And jewelweed ice is great for bruises." She raised an arm and flipped her hand toward the acreage beyond the lodge. "Herb will be driving out there in my Jeep for hours. The sheriff won't have any trouble finding him. We'll charge him with assault and let him cool his wheels in the Bandera jail. Now go."

Forty-Two

Sam and George Tensel were already at the corral when I arrived with my backpack. Sam was about to mount a tall bay horse.

"Sam, could you come help me with these?" I dangled the sixteen-inch Nitrile gloves. "They protect my arms, but they're kind of hard to put on." He looked quizzical. As soon as he came close enough, I told him in a low voice what Herb had done.

"I'd better go get the bastard. He could be our killer."

I grabbed his arm. "Or the killer might be coming on this ride. The sheriff and deputy are on the way. Bertha will tell them where to find Herb. She and Maria are all right. Meredith and I need you here."

He thought about it for what seemed like an eternity, nodded slowly and walked toward his horse. Monty brought George Tensel a bay horse similar to Sam's. He swung up on the saddle in a graceful motion that surprised me. He'd been so sore after his first horseback ride on the ranch. His horse perked up and looked almost as good as Ranger and Monty's horses.

"You do that pretty well for a city slicker," Sam said, "especially one with saddle burns."

"I used to ride as a kid. Just haven't done it in a long time. The burns were superficial. They're about healed. I've got them padded."

Riding a horse was like riding a bicycle. Even if you didn't like it, you never forgot how. Why did George previously pretend he knew nothing about riding horses?

Monty held the reins of a dapple-gray mare for Selma. She eyed the creature with misgivings. “I’m not too crazy about animals.”

Monty motioned for her to come to the right side of the horse and told her to grab the saddle horn. When she tried to put her foot in the stirrup, the horse snorted and side-stepped away from her.

“Monty...” I said. He winked at me. George put his hand over his mouth. He and Monty thought encouraging Selma to mount from the wrong side of the horse was pretty funny. Monty had a tight grip on the reins, so the horse wasn’t going anywhere. The second time Selma tried to put her foot in the stirrup, the horse moved sideways and did its business. She stepped in it.

“Aghhh! Why didn’t you tell me that was there?” She shook her boot frantically, but the soft substance stuck.

We managed not to laugh. I was afraid Selma would start crying.

Ranger cleared his throat to mask a chuckle. “Go over there and swipe your boot on that dry grass,” he told her. “It’ll wipe it off. When we saddle ’em, they get nervous with anticipation. That’s what happens. Out on the trail, the stuff is flat and dry like a Frisbee. If you step on a dry horse patty, it don’t matter.”

“Aw, shucks, I forgot,” Monty told Selma. “Old Cricket here likes to be mounted from her left side. Come on over here. She’ll be all right.” Monty stood there holding the bridle shank. Cricket behaved admirably, not moving a muscle while Selma climbed on to the saddle with her lips quivering.

Our suitemates sauntered up to the corral, all talking at once. Ranger gestured toward Millie.

“I picked Peanut out for you,” he said. Millie quaked toward the ancient black horse whose saddle had a huge horn. Ranger probably figured Millie would eventually grab it. Peanut looked half dead to me...just what Millie needed.

Ranger steered Jangles to a brown horse that didn’t look big enough to carry her. She smiled at Ranger while she hoisted herself onto the saddle. Her poncho practically covered the animal. Her mount, feeling a substantial foreign object on his back, kept turning his head to bite it. Each time he swiveled his head, Jangles squealed.

Ranger and Monty conferred and decided to put Jangles on a bigger horse. They helped her dismount, led her to Moose and hoisted her up. Moose started blowing air out his nose as though he was determined to deflate both himself and his rider.

When Stoney approached the dapple-gray horse they gave her, the horse laid its ears back. The animal might have been perturbed by her husky voice or startled by the silver gleaming from her belt. Once Stoney mounted, the horse backed up, snorting. She yelled "Whoa!" and pulled back on the reins, which didn't help. Monty told her not to do that. He said the horse would settle down once we started moving. I thought Stoney might eventually grab her saddle horn, too.

River Rat slouched up. They gave him a brown horse with a long black mane that hung forward like Rat's hair. I imagined the wranglers shared some chuckles matching up that pair.

Ranger and Monty assigned Meredith to a palomino named Chauncey. Having ridden English saddle horses, she sat straight with her toes barely in the stirrups and the reins held lightly in her hands.

"I rode Chauncey yesterday morning," she said. "This horse can really run. I love it."

My horse, Sparky, a tall bay like Sam's, looked pretty perky. Monty held him while I swung myself up. I'd learned to ride as a child at Aunt Novena and Uncle Fred's farm outside Chicago. I tried to emulate the way Meredith sat her horse, but I had to hold the reins in my left hand. My right one was sore from the wire cut, even under my glove. Ranger and Monty glanced over.

"You left-handed?" Monty asked.

"Ambidextrous."

They looked perplexed.

Wayne Rickoff appeared and strode over to the horse Monty held for him, a sedate black gelding. I surmised the wranglers didn't want Rickoff and his horse to become irritable at the same time. At least the veteran wasn't carrying a rifle or shotgun. I wondered if he'd hidden a pistol in his backpack.

Sunny appeared and went straight to a muscular black gelding, Tonto, and mounted. He appeared to have ridden him before. Tonto had powerful chest muscles and the stocky legs of a quarter horse. Sunny had probably bought him at a rodeo.

Ranger lined us up single file. There were thirteen riders, an ominous number. Ranger said we'd keep the horses to a walk. We might let them trot, but we weren't going to gallop. As Ranger led off, Vicki's horse whinnied from the stables. I tightened my grip on the reins and hugged the horse with my thighs.

Behind Ranger rode Stoney, Jangles and George Tensel. The wranglers must have thought George was a good enough horseman to back up the two women.

Meredith and Millie followed behind George. Then came Sunny, Selma, and River Rat. The wranglers had separated George and Selma by three horses so the couple couldn't fuss at each other.

Rickoff rode behind Rat. Maybe Ranger and Monty figured that if Rickoff started shooting, Rat might as well be in front of him. I got the feeling nobody liked Rat much.

Sam rode behind Rickoff. Did the wranglers sense that Sam might have to keep Rickoff in check? I rode behind Sam, and Monty brought up the rear.

The trouble with trail rides is that the leader rides real slow. Plodding along gets boring. It was totally quiet except for an occasional horse snort. I heard something padding through the brush several yards off the trail, probably a white-tailed deer. It sounded bigger, though, like the cow we'd seen on the first day. I knew Herb was with the goats. The deputy had probably already cuffed him.

I decided to liven things up.

"Ranger, are there many bobcats around here?" I practically had to shout, since he rode up front. My voice stirred the horses. I heard a few snickers and "Whoas." My horse walked faster. From the corners of my eyes, I could see Monty's horse prancing from side to side behind me.

"Easy," Monty said, "Easy."

Since Ranger was the wire expert, I added, "One of those bobcats wired to the dining hall ceiling sure did look different this morning."

Ranger shouted back, "We have a slew of bobcats around here. They kill too many quail. Sometimes we have to shoot the cats."

Meredith must have sensed I was trying to stir something up. She wanted to help. "Isn't killing bobcats strictly regulated in Texas?"

Since we'd stirred the hornet's nest, Sam decided to stick in a probe. "You don't shoot many bobcats, do you, Ranger? You just wire them up. Rickoff's the one who shoots them. You still go to the national forest to shoot 'em, Rickoff, or do you slaughter 'em all here?"

"I'll shoot whatever I want, wherever I want, you son-of-a-bitch." Rickoff drew a pistol from inside his shirt and shot in the air.

Stoney's dapple-gray horse froze with its ears back. "Whoa," Stoney shouted, yanking the reins to her chest. Her horse staggered backward and would have crashed on its hindquarters except that Moose's head broke the fall.

Moose bit Stoney's horse on the rear. When Stoney's horse whinnied and danced sideways, she screeched and grabbed the horse's neck.

Then Moose reared. I was surprised he could lift his front legs that high carrying Jangles. The straps on her backpack were stretched, so when Moose angled up, the straps broke. Jangles' backpack slipped off and hit George Tensel's horse square on the nose. George's horse thrashed around with its head bobbing. George cursed, but he managed to stay on.

Spooked and disoriented, George's horse angled sideways into the brush and flushed a covey of quail. Whooshing and flapping, wild, raucous quail fluttered up from their brushy hiding place, wings thrashing noisily toward the sky. Their frantic commotion scared the bejeebers out of the horses and riders. My horse backed away from the flurry, but I caught a glimpse of another horse and rider beyond the bedlam, mostly obscured by brush. Who was that? My heart stopped.

Stoney's horse, thoroughly unnerved, leaped forward and tore for the stables. Jangles' horse bolted in pursuit. Both women, bowed over like pretzels, grabbed their saddle horns.

George controlled his horse well enough to aim for Selma, who was screeching at the flapping quail. "This is getting crazy," he shouted. "Follow the other horses!" He grabbed her horse's reins, yanked its head toward the stables, then swatted the animal on the rear. Her horse, Cricket, jumped sideways, then leaped forward and started to run. Selma, already clutching the saddle horn, hunched over and bounded away screaming.

Millie saw George coming toward her. She squealed, dropped the reins, humped over and gripped the horn. Her horse charged toward the stables before George even reached her.

River Rat, weighing the options of dealing with crazed, thrashing horses, Rickoff's gunfire or a fast dash to the stables, kicked his horse and followed the women. He made a wrong turn before he hit the open field. Neither he nor his horse saw the oak tree looming ahead. The horse swerved at the last minute and missed the tree. But a branch caught Rat under the chin, lifting him off the saddle. He hung suspended while his horse charged ahead. Then he dropped to the dirt, unconscious.

Ranger yelled to Meredith, "Let's catch up with them and ride on either side of the pack. Try to slow 'em all down so nobody gets hurt. Monty, you stay here with the others." Ranger and Meredith raced off.

Sam slid off his horse and drew his pistol. He didn't relish being a target for Rickoff.

I slipped off my horse.

Sunny and Monty jumped off their horses. The animals raced toward the stables. Heads disappeared behind juniper bushes.

George, the only person still mounted, yelled curses between trying to soothe his horse with calm words.

He shouted, "Monty! Where are you, you little bastard?"

Monty didn't answer.

George yelled at Monty again. "Why'd you fiddle with the damn bobcat, you little weasel?" George's horse tried to pitch his frenzied rider, but George pulled one rein wide to make the horse circle. "Damn horse."

Just as his horse started to settle down, a round petrified cow patty sailed toward George from somewhere on my right. I remembered Monty's amazing accuracy when he threw up clay targets for Rickoff. Monty apparently didn't like George calling him names.

I wondered if Rickoff was aiming his gun at one of the men. Where was Sam?

The cow patty Frisbee hit George's horse on the nostrils. After being clobbered with Jangles' backpack, his nose must be getting pretty sore. The animal pawed the air.

George made a valiant effort to stay mounted, but he slid off backwards and hit the sod like a fat sack of meal. When he moaned and tried to get up, Monty pelted him with a series of petrified patties.

"I should have known better than to deal with you, you little S.O.B.!" George shouted, dodging to escape the barrage. The next missile that flew at him was a rock that smashed against his temple. He roared in pain and fell over, silent.

When I rose to take a peek at George, a cow patty zinged past my right ear. I dropped to the ground.

"Pssst. Over here." The voice came from my left. I heard the hiss of a snake and froze. I saw Sunny crawling toward me on his belly, dragging his backpack. I'd have bet my laptop he'd hidden a stunned snake in his pack.

I made a snap judgment that the snake wasn't meant for me and tried to scoot toward Sunny. Somebody grabbed my feet and pulled me backwards through the underbrush. The long gloves kept my arms from being slashed. I bounced by a stump, grabbed it and held on with all my strength.

The assailant crawled up on my back and flattened me in the dirt. Spikes from his spurs ripped against my ankles. Leather and sweat filled my nostrils. The wild man pulled his body higher on top of me, knocking the breath out of me. When his arm slid under my neck, I smelled a vile, sugary odor. He clamped a hand over my mouth. Putrid hair lapped against my cheek. I heard a knife unsheathe.

"Don't move."

The point of a blade scratched the back of my neck.

"Anybody moves closer, I'll cut her head off."

I whimpered.

"Shut up. Everybody clear out. I want to hear boots movin'. Now! Get over here, Monty. Let's take care of this bitch and get out of here."

From the corner of my eye, I saw Monty's boots. I heard a rustling sound behind him, caught a glimpse of a snake wriggling furiously toward us and prayed that its mouth was wired shut.

I felt a scream coming and bit my lip. The crazed man on my back wouldn't hesitate to slit me open.

Monty whirled to heave a rock at the writhing snake.

"Over here," Sunny taunted him. "Your aim is off."

Monty stepped back to adjust his aim and almost tripped over us. The wild man on top of me lost his grip and rolled off. I spun the other way.

"Aggie, where are you?" Sam yelled. His head popped above a bush behind his gun.

Sunny motioned for me to crawl toward him.

I made it within arm's reach of Sunny when I heard footsteps crunch toward us through the brush. The crazed man with his knife? Rickoff with his gun? Monty aiming a boulder?

"Don't forget to look down," Sunny shouted to the man stomping toward us. Sunny grabbed the snake's tail and slung it toward the approaching boots. Monty squealed and jumped two feet off the ground. When he landed, he took off running and nearly knocked down my attacker. The creep regained his footing and struggled to race after Monty. I recognized him; he was a biker from Bandera. His tight leather pants slowed him down. I threw a petrified patty at him and almost connected.

Sam and Rickoff popped up yards away with their pistols aimed at Monty and his friend.

"Shoot to their right," Sam yelled to Rickoff. "I'll shoot left."

It didn't take many shots before the two men stopped running. Monty raised his arms.

"Okay. Okay. Don't shoot me!" he shrieked. "I'm not movin'. Where's the damn snake?"

"Better keep still, Monty," Sunny hollered. "Snakes aim for movement."

Monty froze like alabaster ice.

"Think we ought to shoot 'em, Rickoff?" Sam asked.

There was a nasty pause. "Naw," Rickoff said. "They ain't worth it."

Sam grabbed handcuffs from his backpack.

"You a cop?" said Monty. "I'll be...You ain't going to let that snake bite me, are you?"

"I'm going to put him in the cell with you and your friend here." Sam tossed a rope to Rickoff. "Go tie up George Tensel. When he comes to, we're going to chat with him and these sleaze balls about a bobcat."

Forty-Three

When George regained consciousness, Sam and Rickoff stood him up and tied the three men, putting the smelly cowboy biker between George and Monty. Sam left two feet of rope between each man. He asked the newcomer his name, the man I'd spotted riding through the brush.

"Currin Dowdy," he grumbled, staring at the ground, his putrid hair flopping forward.

Having smelled him at close range when he flattened me in the dirt, I knew Dowdy must be one of the characters from Texarita's who liked Black Jack's Beard Lube.

Sam grabbed bottled water from a backpack and splashed water in River Rat's face to revive him. He stood Rat up between George and Dowdy and draped Rat's arms around their necks. The scoundrels were obliged to hold Rat up to keep themselves from falling down. George, Rat, Dowdy and Monty made an unforgettable foursome of pathetic specimens.

"If you let him fall," Sam said, "I'll tie him to you."

Rickoff held his gun on them. I noticed the pistol he held was larger than Sam's Glock. With his jaw clinched, Rickoff stood spread-legged in shooter stance, both hands folded around the pistol grip and eyes focused just above the sight. I hoped he didn't decide to shoot them all. Sam didn't seem perturbed by Rickoff.

When Sam came over to me, I was sitting on a stump tying a Nitrile glove around my ankle.

"Are you okay?"

"The creep scratched my leg with his spur. I'll be all right."

"You sure started something with that bobcat remark."

"I did, didn't I?"

"We got these guys, thank God. But one of these days, Aggie…." He helped me up, shaking his head like he couldn't believe the chaos I'd launched.

We padded toward the captives. Sam had his eyes on Rickoff.

"Who's the biker/cowboy?" I asked.

"Monty's jailbird friend, Currin Dowdy."

"The cowboy Meredith saw talking to Monty at the corrals?"

"Yep."

"Didn't we see him at Texarita's Grill?"

"We did. He must have followed us to the BVSBar."

While I pondered how Currin Dowdy figured in the mix, and how long Rickoff could keep from shooting somebody, Sam and Rickoff ordered the four men to walk toward the stables.

It was a long walk. There were a few open areas without mesquite and whitebrush, but not many. The whitebrush had grown spikes after the recent rain. George and Monty, walking on the outside, had a hard time protecting their arms from spikes. The three dragged Rat's close-to-dead weight between them. Having been recently knocked out cold, Rat was too goofy to help much.

Rickoff followed close behind the four men with his gun aimed at them. Sam walked a few paces in back of Rickoff, pointing his Baby Glock at the ground.

"Since you guys like to work together," Sam called to the captives, "I thought I'd give you another chance."

Sunny and I followed them, walking through open spaces whenever we could.

I'd figured out that Monty, using his skill for accurately throwing projectiles, must have heaved a rock at Vicki's horse to make it pitch. Her horse had danced, creating the first batch of horseshoe marks on the trail. But Vicki had apparently stayed mounted.

At that point, Monty must have reverted to a backup plan using the wire, rope and animal hair I found on the trail. Monty would have needed a partner to devise the plan. That's where George Tensel came in.

I scooted ahead of Sunny and sidled up next to Sam. "Are we going to interrogate them at the corrals?"

"We? I don't usually team up with somebody who starts a ruckus that almost gets us killed."

"I'm sorry." I needed to explain. "I was trying to needle Vicki's attacker while we had everybody together. We could have ridden all morning without learning a thing."

"Right."

"I know stuff about the rope and the snake and Vicki," I said.

"I think I've figured it out."

"Probably. But there are crucial elements... and you need documentation. Meredith brought a tape recorder to record information for her articles. We could use that."

He stopped. "Agatha, this is a matter for the law. I'm turning these guys over to the Bandera sheriff."

I grabbed his arm and kept walking. I didn't want to lag too far behind. He had to keep his Glock within range.

Stretching my neck, I whispered in his ear. "You're here undercover without SAPD's sanction. You asked Joaquin at the crime lab to evaluate evidence samples. If you get these creeps' confessions on tape, you'll have proof they tried to murder Vicki. It will exonerate you from those other nasty details, like going it alone. Like not working with local law enforcement."

"I'll think about it." He shook off my hand and marched ahead. My leg ached where the spur had dug in. My feet itched so much it was hard to keep up. Fortunately, I thought the urushiol sap on my poison ivy patches had finally petered out.

I was dying to learn exactly what George had done and why he wanted to kill Vicki Landsdale. I could hear him panting from ten feet away. I hoped he didn't have a heart attack before we could question him.

We finally reached the clearing near the stables. Somebody had opened the corral and let the horses in, including the ones we'd been riding, and closed the gate. Still saddled, they munched on bales of hay, oblivious to the recent trauma.

Meredith and Ranger were trying to comfort riders who'd dashed to the stables. Jangles was a mess. Her arms had new scratches from galloping through the brush, and her hair looked like a bird's nest. Ranger asked her if she was okay. When he promised to make her another wire sculpture, she almost purred.

Millie lay prostrate on the ground. Meredith and Stoney sat on either side of her.

"You're going to be okay," Stoney said. "You can move your arms and legs, so you know everything works. Now you just need to sit up." Millie looked like she was in shock. She didn't even struggle to help them lift her.

"I'm never leaving Dallas again," she croaked.

Selma sat on a log, crying. "I can't believe George hit my horse like that. It ran the whole way home with me trying to hang on." When she saw George, Monty, and the grubby cowboy coming through the brush dragging River Rat, she stopped sniffling.

"Is everybody okay here, Ranger?" Sam called. Ranger nodded.

"We had a few mishaps on the trail," Sam said. "Ranger, why don't you walk the ladies to their cabins? We'll follow in a few minutes." He undraped Rat from Monty, Dowdy and George, keeping his back to the others so they couldn't see that the three culprits were tied together. He sat those three on a log and motioned Rickoff to keep an eye on them. His trusting Rickoff put me on edge.

"Ranger," Sam said, "take River Rat with you when you walk the ladies home. Drop him off at his cabin. Sunny can give you a hand. We'll be along shortly." Ranger seemed so relieved that nobody got hurt, he'd have done anything Sam said.

It looked like Sam wanted to question George, Monty and Dowdy at the corrals where nobody else would hear. Except for Meredith and me, of course.

It appeared Sam was going to let Rickoff hang around, too. I ran over to Meredith. "Tell the others you'll go on ahead," I whispered. "Grab your tape recorder and sneak back here. Make sure nobody sees you. You're about to get a scoop."

Forty-Four

The women tromped toward their cabins accompanied by Ranger, Rat and Sunny. When they were far enough away to be out of earshot, Sam turned to Rickoff. "Can you get more rope? We need to re-tie these guys."

Rickoff went to get rope from the horse barn. I hoped he didn't come back carrying a shotgun. While Sam held his pistol on Monty, George, and Currin Dowdy, I sat quietly off to one side. Sam hadn't banished me yet. If Rickoff didn't explode, I might have a good chance to hear the culprits' stories.

Monty scoured the ground with his eyes. He seemed more worried about snakes than about Sam. I heard him let out a sigh when Sunny left. George was in such lousy shape, he was still panting.

By the time Meredith returned with her tape recorder, Sam and Rickoff had re-tied the three men. Meredith handed the recorder to Sam and came to sit by me. Sam gave the two of us a "keep quiet" look before he clicked on the machine.

Sam gave his name, title, date and location. Then he turned to Monty. "Tell us who you are and what you're doing at the BVSBar Ranch."

"Uh. Monty Malone, Assistant Wrangler. Address... uh... bunkhouse by the stables, BVSBar Ranch, Bandera, Texas."

Sam turned to Currin Dowdy and had him state his name and current address. "You were in jail with Monty Malone?"

"Yeah. Ain't that the luck."

"Meredith Laughlin overheard you say that Monty Malone killed somebody with a knife. Who did he kill?"

"Nobody, fer as I knew. He'd had so many knife fights in them gangs, I figured he musta kilt somebody."

"Then why did you tell him he killed someone?"

"When I got outta the pen, they weren't hiring ex-cons, even for the rodeo circuit. I heard y'all talkin' at Texarita's about goin' to some dude ranch. I followed you and found out Monty had got himself this here job. Figured I might get me one."

"When Monty told you Ranger wasn't hiring new wranglers, did you try to blackmail Monty to get yourself hired?"

"Right. Alls I know is wranglin'. If I cain't do that, there ain't nothing else."

"You almost killed that lady." He pointed over at me. "That's assault. Attempted murder." Sam's face turned an angry shade of red.

"I didn't aim to kill nobody," Dowdy said.

Sam took a couple of deep breaths and looked over at me. I gave him a thumbs-up.

He turned to Monty. "Where were you the night Vicky Landsdale rode her horse on the BVSBar Ranch trail by the river, the night she was found lying on that trail?"

"I'd gone down to the trail earlier and was hidin' in the brush. We planned it, me and George here." He flicked his thumb in George Tensel's direction. "He knew I could get rope from the barn and wire from Ranger to drag the bobcat, then put the critter back on the ceiling."

George Tensel stared at the dirt.

"You took a stuffed bobcat down from the dining room ceiling of the lodge, here at the BVSBar Ranch?" Sam asked.

"Yeah," Monty said. "While everybody was eatin' dinner outside, I tied wire around the cat's neck, hooked it to a rope, took it to the horse trail and hid it in the brush. I laid the rope across the trail in a crevice and smoothed dirt over it so nobody'd see it. I'd yank it across from the other side and spook Vicki's horse. Since everybody ate grub out on the patio that night, I figured nobody'd miss the cat in the dining room."

"Whose idea was it to scare Vicki's horse?"

Sam wanted to record the complete identity of the person who instigated Vicki's fall.

"I told ya. It was his... George Tensel." Monty jerked his head toward George. "Good thing he thought of that cat. When I threw the rock, it spooked the horse, but that little citified twit rode well enough to stay on. Damnedest thing."

"The little twit... you're referring to Vicki Landsdale?"

Sam's law school training was apparent.

"Yeah," Monty said. "Shore 'nuf, I had to yank the bobcat across the trail in front of her horse."

"Was that when Vicki Landsdale fell off?"

"Yeah. The horse went nuts and pitched her. She hit her head on them rocks."

"Did somebody tell you to spook Vicki Landsdale's horse so she'd fall off?"

Sam had to nail down the perpetrator and the facts. He must have testified for the prosecution enough times to know the details of a case had to be airtight for a jury to convict the guilty party.

"Like I said, George Tensel here told me to spook Vicki's horse. 'Course I didn't like the girl noway. Ranger was nuts about her and she treated him like he wadn't there. Vicki knew I didn't like her. I figured if she ever changed her mind about Ranger, she'd wrap him around her li'l finger and tell him to dump me first thing. I had the best deal anybody ever seen 'round here. I wadn't about to let no little twit louse it up. When George told me he was figurin' a way to make this here ranch lose money so he could buy it cheap, I reckoned I had me a partner."

I nodded. When I witnessed how well George rode his horse, I suspected he liked ranches better than he let on. Sam saw me nodding and gave me a warning look. I pressed my lips together.

"George Tensel," Sam said, "you wanted to buy the BVSBar Ranch? Haven't you told everybody here you hate ranches?"

"Yeah. But I know what they're worth. Eighteen hundred acres in the heart of the Hill Country? I'd been trying to buy choice real estate like this for years. Couldn't touch the price. Decided maybe I could get this one cheap."

The starch and bravado seemed to have gone out of George. I was glad he was pathetically out of shape. His hike through the brush must have prompted him to get the whole ordeal behind him.

"I sure could use some water," George said.

"I imagine you could," Sam said. "You thought you could buy the BVSBar Ranch cheap? Why was that?"

"Old Bertha would never sell. The owners died and left it to her, but they fixed it so she couldn't sell the ranch unless it was losing serious money and she couldn't run it anymore. She could live on it forever, but title to the ranch would go straight to the Nature Conservancy."

"I overheard you tell your wife Selma," Sam said, "to call the Nature Conservancy. What was that call about?"

George glared at Sam, but he knew better than to chastise Sam for eavesdropping on his conversation.

"I just wondered," George said, "if they thought Bertha Sampson might be ready to give up and let the conservancy have the ranch."

I knew there was more to that story. I was dying to tell Sam how Maria overheard George Tensel tell Bertha he was determined to buy this ranch. But I knew better than to interrupt.

Monty piped up. "George figured a little tragedy at the ranch would make people stop comin', at least for a while. The ranch would lose money, and the price would go down. That was okay with me. George said someday he'd be boss, and he'd keep me and Ranger on. We'd be head guys."

George shot daggers at Monty. He was probably wondering why he ever got mixed up with this character.

I shook my head. George Tensel tried to kill poor Vicki Landsdale to get his hands on this ranch. He didn't even like ranches. Yet he'd kill an innocent young girl just to satisfy his greed. I slapped my hand over my mouth to keep from blurting my disgust.

"How did you know," Sam asked George, "what the former owners set up regarding this ranch?"

"I had a lawyer friend research the title and dig out some information," George said.

"Was anybody else involved in the attack on Vicki Landsdale?" Sam asked.

I knew Sam was thinking about Sunny Barlow. I simply couldn't keep quiet any longer.

"Pssst," I said to Sam, motioning him to punch the pause button on the recorder. He glared at me with a this-better-be-good expression. I scampered over and whispered in his ear. I thought I knew the answer about Sunny, but I needed to talk to Sunny again while Sam got the other men's confessions on tape.

When I finished telling Sam what I knew, he nodded and clicked the recorder on to resume questioning the men.

I motioned for Meredith to stay put and took off running for Sunny Barlow's cabin.

Forty-Five

I knocked on Sunny's door. When he opened it, he'd washed off his makeup. His eyes, set in his freshly scrubbed face, looked haunted. Despite sunken eyes and the white scar streaking down his jaw, his black curly hair and cobalt blue eyes made him startlingly handsome.

"May I come in?

He nodded. I walked past him and sat in one of his cabin chairs. He followed me with his eyes but didn't say anything. He must have sensed I was bringing news he didn't want to hear.

"George Tensel and Monty Malone conspired to make Vicki's horse throw her," I said. "Sam and Wayne Rickoff have them tied up. Sam is questioning them now at the corrals and taping their confessions on Meredith's recorder." I paused to let him digest what I'd said. He looked stunned and didn't respond. I had shocked him. I might as well tell him the rest.

"A biker/cowboy named Currin Dowdy, Monty's former jail mate, showed up to blackmail Monty into helping him get a job at the ranch. Sam's got Dowdy tied up, too."

Sunny walked to his bureau. He was apparently trying to make sense of what I told him. He sniffed and wiped the back of his hand across his mouth. "Why would George Tensel want to hurt Vicki?"

"He wanted to cause an accident at the ranch— scare customers away so he could buy the property cheap. He got Monty to help him. Monty drew a stuffed bobcat across the trail in front of Vicki's horse so it would pitch her."

Sunny slammed his fist on the bureau so hard, the makeup pots danced.

"I know, I know," I said. "It was pointless and stupid and cruel. I don't know if Monty and George meant to kill Vicki, but if she dies, they'll be charged with her murder."

He turned his back. I heard muffled sounds and thought he was trying not to cry.

"Why are Sam and Meredith questioning them?" he mumbled.

"Sam is a San Antonio homicide detective who came to the ranch to vacation with Meredith and me. He saw no reason to identify himself as a law officer, but when Vicki was thrown, Sam started secretly investigating. Meredith is helping him."

He kept his back to me.

"If it's any consolation," I said, "I know Vicki loved you. She lit up when you were around. She knew she'd found her mate, another kind soul who wanted to help people."

He whirled and stared at me. "Why would that bastard Monty want to harm Vicki?"

"He thought she posed a threat to his chance to manage the ranch with Ranger. When Monty saw a chance to partner with George Tensel and get rid of Vicki, he thought it would secure his job as Ranger's assistant. Monty wanted to make it look like you were responsible for Vicki's accident—I'm not sure why—by spattering your face paint on rocks where Vicki fell."

Sunny sagged into the other chair and held his head in his hands. He finally looked up.

"I got off track in high school," he said. "My teenage gang tangled with Monty's bunch. Monty cut my face. That's how I got the scar. Rickoff attacked me later at the vet rodeo, but this"—he pointed to the scar—"was Monty's work."

"I lost a lot of blood and spent time in the hospital. Monty went to jail for what he did. I lost hope of ever having a better life. When Monty got a job at this ranch and realized I already worked here, he probably thought I'd devise a plan to send him back to jail."

"I see. If Monty got rid of you and Vicki, he'd eliminate any obstacles that might prevent him from being a big shot here with Ranger Travis."

"I guess that's right," he said. "I think Monty suspected I had something to do with snakes popping up at odd times." He grinned. "I sure loved seeing him jump like a frog out there in that field."

We both chuckled.

"I thought if I hassled Monty enough," Sunny said, "he'd go find another job, him and Wayne Rickoff both. I wouldn't have to keep looking at either one of their sorry faces."

"I thought Wayne Rickoff cut your face at the rodeo." I struggled to keep concentrating on Sunny because I kept picturing Rickoff out there with Sam, clutching that gun. "After Rickoff shaved off his beard, did you recognize him at the cookout as the vet who attacked you?"

"I was startled by how different he looked," Sunny said, "but I already knew he was the vet who came after me. When he jumped me at the rodeo, I was an adult, so I understood why he did it.

"In high school, after I got out of the hospital, I started wearing clown makeup and doing kids' parties after school. Funny thing was, I found I liked making kids happy. I worked as a rodeo clown even after I graduated. I'd have gone to college, but I didn't think I could face anybody without makeup to cover up this scar." He touched his face. "Vicki convinced me I didn't need makeup."

"You definitely don't need it. With your looks and personality and singing talent, you have a lot to contribute."

"I'd like to try college. I saved a lot of money for the Caribbean, but we... I won't be going now. We were going to Saba. They call it Sa-bay.... I could save more money by working here until Bertha finds somebody to take my place. Then I could enroll to study psychology. Maybe help troubled teens."

"Vicki would like that."

"Yeah. I think she would."

I patted Sunny's arm and left him to try and deal with the pain of all that had happened.

* * *

I walked back to my cabin. Anger and greed ruined so many lives. You could possess all the knowledge in the universe and never comprehend how people's self-centeredness could motivate them to take another person's life.

From talking to the suspects, Sam had undoubtedly already discovered Sunny Barlow wasn't involved in Vicki's accident. I'd reassure him about Sunny later.

Right now, I was curious about the place where Sunny and Vicki planned to go. I slipped into our cabin, powered up my computer and searched "Caribbean Islands." The tiny dot on the map I'd seen turned out to be Saba, a Dutch, five-square-mile island in the northeastern Caribbean, north of St. Kitts. It had four small villages and two banks. I remembered the number on Vicki's note and clicked one of the banks—the Windward Islands Bank.

Forty-Six

I walked to the lodge to tell Bertha how Monty and George Tensel conspired to cause Vicki's fall and about Currin Dowdy.

"Bastards," Bertha said. "Who's Currin Dowdy?" After I told her, I said I had questions.

"Why did you keep telling us Vicki was improving when you knew she could die?"

"There was nothing I could do to help Vicki," Bertha said, "and I couldn't afford to have everybody leave. Today was your last day here. If Vicki died after you returned home, I thought it would be a few days before anybody learned about her death. The longer I could keep the tragedy quiet, the less damage there would be to the ranch." She breathed out a discouraged sigh. "Poor Vicki. She was startin' to feel like my little sister."

"Do you know any more about her condition?"

"Only that she was still unconscious this morning. After I found that out, Herb busted in here."

"If you lose customers, you lose this ranch?"

"Yes. As long as I maintain it as a profitable business, it's mine. If I can just make it here five more years, I'll own it outright."

"Water resurfacing at the old well site should help you save the ranch," I said, watching her reaction.

Bertha's eyes opened wide. "How'd you know about that?"

"I wondered about the Vernons' deaths. When Sam and I did research in town, we located the well on a map, went to find it and stumbled upon the water."

"Then you know Max and Billy Sue died of natural causes, heat stroke aggravated by dehydration."

"Yes."

She looked away as though viewing a window to the past. "When Max and Billy Sue went to the well," she said, "the water had apparently recessed underground. They must have stayed around, hoping to see it resurface. I guess they stayed too long." Her eyes filled with tears. "We can always use jewelweed at the ranch, so I planted some around the well. To mark the spot in their memory."

"Their attorney, Marshall Darren, thought you didn't know until after they died that they changed their wills to leave you this ranch."

"That's right," she said. "I don't think Herb knew either."

I was glad to hear that. Maybe I could quit worrying about whether Bertha or Herb had added diuretics to the couple's thermoses.

A smile unexpectedly played around her mouth. "If I can hang on to this ranch, I'm pretty sure Ranger will stay." She glanced across the dining room to the check-in desk where the wire sculptures were displayed, the ones Ranger made for her. "I better get ready to go on a diet."

If Bertha was successful getting Ranger back, I hoped he turned out to be worth having.

"I do have good news. Meredith can hardly wait to write articles about the ranch—its beauty, the meandering Medina River, Maria's scrumptious food, the activities, Sunny's cookouts and his singing. Her article should entice people to come here."

"That will certainly help. I'll go thank her."

"Actually, if you feel up to it, you might want to go sympathize with Millie, Stoney, and Jangles. They had a pretty rough ride when their horses spooked and charged to the stable. Maybe you could pay the girls' way for a couple of days at the nearest spa if they promise to book a cabin here later?"

Forty-Seven

We walked together toward cabin six, but I walked on ahead to see Selma. Even though she and George argued constantly and seemed to have little in common, I thought I should let her down gently before she saw her husband handcuffed. I knocked on her cabin door.

"Come in." She sat at their table, sniffling. "I still can't believe George whapped my horse on the rump," she said, "and how I managed to stay on that wild creature." She motioned me to a chair.

"I'm glad you're okay," I said, joining her. "I'm afraid I have more bad news about George." When I told her he conspired with Monty Malone to hurt Vicki, and that Sam would hand them over to the Bandera sheriff, she sighed despondently. But she stopped crying. She almost seemed to expect bad news about George.

"When George had me call the Nature Conservancy," she said, "I realized he had designs on this ranch."

I sensed Selma was prepared to deliver up facts about her husband and, for the first time, acknowledge them to herself.

"I'm on the Nature Conservancy's board," she said. "When George started giving the organization money a couple years ago, I found his sudden generosity peculiar. He's never enjoyed parting with money, he laughed at conservation programs and never missed a chance to chide me about being on the board. When he had me call them, I finally realized what was going on."

"What did he want you to find out?"

"Whether Bertha Sampson had indicated to anyone in the organization that the ranch was failing financially and whether she was about to ask the conservancy to take over the property. When I told him nobody had heard from Bertha, I could tell he was disappointed. That's when I realized he wanted this ranch."

"If the ranch went to the conservancy," I asked her, "how could George obtain ownership?"

Her lips thinned into a grim line, as though she was angry at herself. "Various conservancies are set up differently. In this organization, acquired properties are managed by board members or large contributors."

"You and George fit both those requirements."

"Exactly. And now that we've stayed at the BVSBar, George could describe this ranch to the conservancy board in detail. He could eloquently explain why we are the obvious choices to manage this property." She sighed. "He knows I wouldn't be interested in staying here. He'd have free rein."

"The way the Vernons set up their wills, if Bertha can hang on five more years, the ranch becomes hers, and the conservancy can't claim it."

"That explains George's sudden interest in the property," she said. "He's even greedier than I thought. A real predator."

I couldn't disagree. "If he could use the conservancy to get in position to manage the ranch, he'd have five more years to figure out how to acquire ownership."

She leaned back and looked at the ceiling as though seeking answers to her relationship with George. Finally, she spoke. "We've been apart a lot, George and me. Never did understand one another. It's a good thing we never had children."

"What will you do now?"

"I'll have to get a divorce. Maybe I'll take back my maiden name. I might even open a spa. I've dreamed about a ritzy place that uses natural products that don't damage the environment. Of course, it wouldn't have any poisonous plants or nasty creatures in outdoor areas."

"Of course not. Maybe Jangles and her friends can give you tips from the beauty business."

"That would be good. George made so much money, he began making investments and putting them in my name. I can use it to start my business."

"I wonder if a spa in the Hill Country would be successful," I mused aloud.

Forty-Eight

I left Selma to contemplate her future. When I entered our cabin, Meredith was packing. We heard laughter, walked through the breezeway and found Selma and Bertha in the cabin with Jangles, Millie, and Stoney.

"I told 'em I'd treat them to a day at the nearest spa," Bertha said, "but they had better ideas."

They looked like cats that had swallowed canaries and could barely suppress smiles. Meredith and I waited.

"We're going to open a spa here at the ranch." Jangles giggled.

"We're going to be partners," Stoney said. "Millie can keep the books. She's a tight-ass accountant." Millie cut her eyes at Stoney, but she was too excited to stay mad.

"Stoney will fix whatever breaks," Millie said. "And she'll fumigate the place regularly to make sure critters stay out."

Stoney nodded. "I know a builder who can build anything, and I'll help him. Later on, we can update the cabins."

"I told Bertha I'd pay to build the spa," Selma said. "I'd just as soon build it here as anyplace. Here, I won't have to pay rent. I'll sell the house I shared with George and use that money. Since Jangles has been in the beauty business, we can use her expertise to design the spa and beauty shop and won't have to hire a decorator."

Jangles beamed. "We'll have an adorable little shop alongside the spa. Beauty products are big money makers. We'll sell those fabulous backpacks Bertha designed and charge extra for embroidered insignias. Our spa products will be 'Hill Country

Fresh.'" She giggled. "Naturally, we'll sell caftans, jewelry and unique flip-flops."

"And liquid jewelweed in fancy bottles," Bertha added.

Selma continued, "Thirty percent of profits will come to me until the building is paid for. Bertha will get another thirty percent for providing the land. Then we'll split the profits five ways."

"I swore I was through with ranching," said Millie, "but running a business with my friends, where bugs and critters are kept out, sounds good. It can be an oasis from rustic living."

"Absolutely, no critters," Selma said.

We hugged them. Meredith asked Bertha if she'd meet us at the lodge to check out.

We finished packing and loaded our bags into Sam's Caprice. He walked up looking refreshed and pleased with himself and hurled his suitcase into the trunk. We drove to the lodge, checked out and gave Bertha and Maria a final hug.

Forty-Nine

Sunny stood in front watching Sam and Rickoff load George, Monty and Currin Dowdy, handcuffed, into the back of the sheriff's cage car. Deputy Cranton leaned against a second patrol car, watching.

I walked over to Sam. "Another deputy took Herb to jail," he said. "He'll come back later and drive Bertha to retrieve her Jeep."

Sunny, still wearing one of Bertha's backpacks, motioned me over. He sidled close, pulled a crumpled piece of paper from an outside pocket of the backpack and spoke to me in a low voice. "Look at this. I found it in Vicki's cabin. She left me a hurried note, but I thought she meant to say more, so I searched her cabin." He smoothed the paper out for me to read.

Dearest Sunny,

In case we never go to the Caribbean together, use this however you wish. It comes with all my love forever.

Vicki
Windward Islands Bank, Ltd., Saba Island,
Dutch Caribbean. Account #0746.

It was the same number Vicki had scribbled on the note I found. I'd called a Saba Island bank, inquired about opening an account and asked the bank clerk to read me a sample account number. Having studied business and working at banks came in handy, even though it numbed the mind. Vicki had scribbled her account number at Saba's Windward Islands Bank.

I handed the note to Sunny and squeezed his hand.

"I've got one more thing to do," he said, "before I go to San Antonio."

He probably wanted to commiserate with Vicki's parents. I hoped he could convince them Vicki's note meant she intended for him to have her Caribbean funds.

Sunny walked over to Sam, handed him a different note and whispered in his ear. Sam passed the note to the sheriff. The Sheriff and deputy loaded up the three sleazebags to take them to Bandera County Jail.

As the sheriff started the car, Wayne Rickoff walked up with his pistol holstered.

Sunny opened the door to the back seat where the cage separated losers from the law officers in front. He slipped off his backpack, reached in and tossed an open burlap sack into the backseat. The sheriff and deputy drove off with their cargo.

As the car rolled over the cattle guard at the entrance, we could hear the men in the backseat screaming. Monty yelled the loudest.

Sunny and Sam howled with laughter. Wayne Rickoff doubled over laughing. He looked a lot better when he smiled.

Fifty

As we turned toward the main gate, we saw Bertha and Ranger walking toward the corrals, talking.

"I bet they'll be real careful who they hire," Sam said.

"I predict Bertha goes on a strict diet," I said.

We told Sam the girls' plans for the Hill Country spa.

"I'll have Bertha tell Marshall Darren about their plans," he said. "That should enhance the ranch's value and boost Bertha's income. With Darren on her side, Bertha should be able to keep the property."

"Will she be able to re-drill the water well?" I asked.

"Darren thinks the water board will grant her a drilling permit."

We mused in silence as the road curved toward Bandera.

"Wayne Rickoff sure seemed different by the time we left," I said.

"When he got to use his skills for something good," Sam said, "his fury drained out. He asked me what training is involved to become a police officer."

Meredith sat in back with sound buds in her ears, listening to the villains' taped confessions. We weren't far from Bandera when Sam reached across the seat and grabbed my hand. "I have a sudden, overwhelming craving."

"Really?" My eyes grew wide. My heart beat faster.

"I think we need a Bubba Burger."

Meredith and I passed on that option.

* * *

We descended through the hills. The highway was still wide, but instead of mesquite, yucca and cenizo, homes dotted the hillsides. We were back among gas stations, roadside restaurants and billboards. The landscape changed. I wondered if people ever would.

Sam stopped at Meredith's condo and hauled her bags inside. She was eager to start working on her articles.

He drove to my bungalow on Burr Road, and we carried my suitcases inside. After he set the last bag down, he cradled my shoulders and looked at me. "I almost lost you again."

I nodded.

"I don't want to lose you, Aggie. I know that now." He pulled me close and wrapped his arms around me. We stood, savoring the moment. It was wonderful being with him without worrying who might be watching or who might harm us. I didn't have to worry about hiding clues or gaining his trust.

He kissed my cheeks. My lips. My neck.

I looked into his eyes. "Sam, there's something I..."

"Don't say anything. We've come a long way. But we have a long way to go. You and I both know that's true."

My eyes started to fill.

"For now," he said, "let's enjoy being together. There's plenty of time."

He gave me a long, lingering kiss. My resolve melted. All I wanted was to cling to him.

He backed away, grasped my shoulders, pecked me on the nose and left.

Maybe he suspected the truth and didn't want me to confirm it. Maybe he needed time to get used to the idea.

I sighed. Someday I'd have to confess the secret that he reared my beloved daughter. Someday.

But we had time. Plenty of time.

Fifty-One

I stood still until I heard his car pull away. Smiling, I picked up a pile of mail from where it had landed on the floor. I flipped through and stopped at an envelope. It didn't look like a letter to Dear Aggie, yet the handwriting was familiar. I ripped it open.

Dear Aggie,

I wondered whether I'd have the chance to thank you. Yesterday, I remembered what happened. I was awake when he came in. We talked and talked—so much to catch up on. We kissed and promised never to be apart. My parents, standing in the doorway, had heard us talk about healing, about going to college, and about our desire to help kids. They gave us their blessing.

We'll honeymoon on Saba Island. In September, we'll enroll in school. Sunny also sends his love.

Vicki

In Case You Missed the 1st Book in the Series

FIT TO BE DEAD #1

Exercise can be fatal.

Aggie Mundeen, single and pushing forty, fears nothing but middle age. When she moves from Chicago to San Antonio, she decides she better shape up before anybody discovers she writes the column, “Stay Young with Aggie.” She takes Aspects of Aging at University of the Holy Trinity and plunges into exercise at Fit and Firm.

Rusty at flirting and mechanically inept, she irritates a slew of male exercisers, then stumbles into murder. She’d like to impress the investigating detective with her sleuthing skills. But when the killer comes after her, and the health club has to evacuate semi-clad patrons, the detective stalls his investigation. Aggie has to forgo fitness in favor of staying alive.

Lefty Award Finalist for Best Humorous Mystery

"Aggie's wry observations on life, death, and the struggle to whip mind and body into shape make this a delightful read."

_Karen McCullough

Wired for Murder

Aggie Returns to College

SMART, BUT DEAD #3

Academics can be murder.

Aggie Mundeen Mystery (#3)

Skirting forty and appalled by the prospect of descending into middle-age, Aggie Mundeen blasts off to the local university to study the genetics of aging. She is doggedly determined to stay young.

Despite conflicts with her professor, she learns about the Human Genome Project and DNA. When she discovers a dead body, Detective Sam reminds her not to "help" with the investigation. But dangerously curious and programmed to prod, she races to solve the crime, winds up the prime suspect and is on target to become next campus corpse.

Short List: Chanticleer International Book Awards

"A tight mystery, an irrepressible heroine, and superb writing."
_Award-winnng author James W. Ziskin

"Aggie's pluck, humor, and intelligence and loving heart keep her young and make readers smile."
_Award-winning author Carolyn Hart

Destination Vacation: the San Antonio River Walk

RIVER CITY DEAD #4

A vacation in paradise?

Aggie Mundeen, columnist and amateur sleuth, prepares for an idyllic weekend with her love interest, SAPD Detective Sam, at a San Antonio River Walk hotel.

Single for years and pushing forty, she is jittery. She yearns for a weekend away from crime--a fiesta, not a fiasco. But Sam, already at the hotel, calls her. Something is very wrong in their luxury suite. Surprise. Mischief. Murder.

Raven Award Mystery Winner

Killer Nashville Highlighted Book

"River City Dead is peppered with humor and wit and has a nice touch of romance in the plot. The Texas setting and use of Fiesta Week as background give distinctive flavor to this novel. This installment in the Aggie Mundeen series has all the elements of a great cozy mystery. Highly recommended." _*Mystery Tribune*

VISIT THE AUTHOR

Facebook
https://www.facebook.com/authorNancyG.West

Website
https://nancygwest.com

Aggie's Views of her Author
http://nancygwest.com/aggies-blog

Nancy G. West

Nancy G. West was a business major who returned to study English literature and discovered that writing fiction is a lot more fun than accounting. She is the award-winning author of psychological suspense, *Nine Days to Evil*, and the Aggie Mundeen Mystery Series: *Fit to Be Dead, Dang Near Dead, Smart, But Dead,* and *River City Dead.*

The Plunge, a novella bridge to the forthcoming spin-off series, The Aggie Mundeen Lake Mysteries, was a June 2019 selection for ALA's Book Club.

Her recently completed coming-of-age novel features a new adult whose discovery compels him to solve a mystery to save his family.

JOIN A PRIVATE CLUB

To receive special offers, updates, new book releases, and author insights in BOOK NEWS, go to the link below and enter your email address.

https://www.subscribepage.com/a1n3e1

www.ingramcontent.com/pod-product-compliance
Lightning Source LLC
Chambersburg PA
CBHW071524110726
47908CB00003B/939

* 9 7 8 1 7 3 4 1 1 7 5 5 4 *